"*Is this what you want?*"

Fire invaded Stephanie, robbing her of strength.

"How many men have you slept with?" The raw note in Duke's voice abraded her nerves as savagely as his expert caress. With lingering thoroughness he explored the bones of her hip and the sensitive hollow beneath. Stephanie gasped, biting back a moan.

And then she was almost flung across the bed. "Sorry, princess, I was paid to rescue you, not act as your gigolo...."

ROBYN DONALD has always lived in Northland in New Zealand, initially on her father's stud dairy farm at Warkworth, then in the Bay of Islands, an area of great natural beauty, where she lives today with her husband and an ebullient and mostly Labrador dog. She resigned from her teaching position when she found she enjoyed writing romances more, and any time when she's not writing, she spends reading, gardening, traveling and writing letters to keep up with her two adult children and her friends.

Books by Robyn Donald

Don't miss any of our special offers. Write to us at the following address for information on our newest releases.

Harlequin Reader Service
U.S.: 3010 Walden Ave., P.O. Box 1325, Buffalo, NY 14269
Canadian: P.O. Box 609, Fort Erie, Ont. L2A 5X3

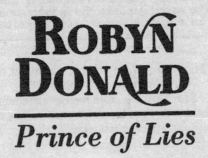

ROBYN DONALD

Prince of Lies

Harlequin Books

TORONTO • NEW YORK • LONDON
AMSTERDAM • PARIS • SYDNEY • HAMBURG
STOCKHOLM • ATHENS • TOKYO • MILAN
MADRID • WARSAW • BUDAPEST • AUCKLAND

For Sharon Wade Beeson, who asked,
"And what about Stephanie?"
And for Sam McGredy, rose breeder extraordinaire.
For his kindness and for making the world a more
beautiful place.

ISBN 0-373-11783-3

PRINCE OF LIES

First North American Publication 1995.

Copyright © 1995 by Robyn Donald.

This edition published by arrangement with Harlequin Books S.A.

® and TM are trademarks of the publisher. Trademarks indicated with
® are registered in the United States Patent and Trademark Office, the
Canadian Trade Marks Office and in other countries.

Printed in U.S.A.

CHAPTER ONE

SOMBRE fir trees crowded against the small stone crypt constructed in the living rock of the mountain, concealing it from all but the keenest eyes.

The man who threaded his way so quietly that even the deer didn't sense his presence had such eyes, strange, colourless eyes that refracted light like shattered glass. At a muffled sound in the still silence he froze, his big body somehow blending into the gloom, that fierce gaze searching through the trees and up the mountainside.

A hundred years ago an eccentric English gentleman had built a little castle high in the Swiss Alps, but it was his wife who decided that the estate needed something extra, a romantically outrageous touch to set it off properly. A couple of ruined follies sufficed for dramatic impact in the woods, but the *pièce de résistance* was the crypt, never intended to be used, constructed solely to induce the right mood.

During the past century the carefully laid path had become overgrown, scarcely noticeable, but the crypt had been built by good Victorian tradesmen, and it still stood in all its Gothic gloom, the rigid spikes of an elaborately detailed iron grille barring steps that led down to a solid wooden door.

Frozen in a purposeful, waiting immobility, ears and eyes attuned to the slightest disturbance, the man decided that as an example of the medieval sensibility admired by many Victorians the hidden crypt was perfect. Not his style, but then, his self-contained pragmatism was utterly at variance with the romantic attitudes of a century before.

In spite of the fugitive noise that had whispered across his ears, no birds shouted alarm, no animals fled between the trees. His penetrating gaze lingered a moment on stray beams of the hot Swiss sun fighting their way through the dense foliage.

He hadn't seen anyone since entering the wood and his senses were so finely honed that he'd have known if he'd been followed, or if the crypt was being watched. The waiting was a mere formality. However, when a man lived on his wits it paid to have sharp ones, and the first thing he'd learned was to trust nothing, not even his own reactions.

A small, bronze butterfly settled on one broad shoulder. Not until the fragile thing had danced off up the nearest sunbeam did he move, and then it was soundlessly, with a smooth flowing grace very much at variance with his size. Within moments he was standing at the dark opening in the shoulder of the mountain.

The iron door looked suitably forbidding, but the old-fashioned lock that would have been, for all its ornate promise, ridiculously easy to pick, had been superseded by a modern one, sleek, workmanlike, somehow threatening. After a cursory glance he fished in his pocket and pulled out a ring of keys. No clink of metal pierced the silence. Selecting one, he inserted it, and as the key twisted and the lock snickered back a look of savage satisfaction passed over his hard, intimidating face.

He didn't immediately accept the mute invitation. Instead, his eyes searched the stone steps that led down to another door, this one made of sturdy wood. For several seconds the cold, remote gaze lingered on what could have been scuff marks.

Eventually, with the measured, deliberate calculation of a predator, he turned his head. Again his eyes scanned the fir trees and the barely visible path through them, then flicked up the side of the mountain. Only then did he push the iron door open.

Although he knew it had been oiled, he half expected a dramatic shriek of rusty hinges. One corner of his straight mouth tilted in mordant appreciation of the horror films he and his friends used to watch years ago, when he was as innocent as he'd ever been.

Moving without noise or haste, he slipped through the narrow opening between the iron door and the stone wall, relocked the door, and turned, his back pressed against the damp, rough-hewn stone. Now, caught between the grille and the wooden door, he was most vulnerable to ambush.

Still no prickle of danger, no obscure warning conveyed by the primitive awareness that had saved his life a couple of times. Keeping well to the side where the shadows lay deepest, he walked noiselessly down the steps. Some part of his brain noted the chill that struck through his clothes and boots.

A different key freed the wooden door; slowly, he pushed it open, his black head turning as a slight scrabble sounded shockingly in the dank, opaque darkness within.

'It's all right, Stephanie,' he said in a voice pitched to reach whoever was in the crypt. Grimly, he locked the door behind him. A hitherto concealed torch sent a thin beam of light slicing through the blackness to settle on a long box, eerily like a coffin, that rested on the flagstones. The man played the light on to the box until the keyhole glittered. For the space of three heartbeats he stood motionless, before, keys in hand, he approached the box.

Inside her prison she was blind, and earplugs made sure she could hear little. However, another sense had taken over, an ability to feel pressure, to respond somehow to the presence of another living being. For the last few minutes she had known he was near.

Almost certainly he was one of the two men who had abducted her on the road back to the chalet. The memory of those terrifying moments kept her still and quiet, her shackled limbs tense against the narrow sides of the box.

After the initial horrified incredulity she had fought viciously, desperation clearing her brain with amazing speed so that she was able to use every move Saul had taught her. She'd managed to get in some telling blows, scratching one's face badly as she'd torn off his Balaclava. She had been trying for his eyes, but a blow to her head had jolted her enough to put off her aim.

Not badly enough, however, to stop her from crooking her fingers again and gouging at his face, so clearly seen in the moonlight.

Then the second man had punched her on the jaw.

Two days later the man whose face she'd seen had hit her again in exactly the same place when she'd refused to read the newspaper.

Half-mad with terror, convinced that she was going to die in the makeshift coffin, she had managed to shake her head when he'd forced her upright and thrust the newspaper in her hand, demanding that she say the headlines.

She'd known what he was doing. Saul must want some reassurance that she was alive before he paid any ransom. The torches that had blazed into her eyes had made it very clear that her assailant intended to video her.

Her refusal had made her gaoler angry, and he'd threatened to withhold the food and water he'd brought. Still she'd balked, folding her mouth tightly over the cowardly words fighting to escape, words that were pleas for freedom, craven offers to pay him anything he wanted if only he would let her go.

So he'd hit her, carefully choosing the site of the bruise he'd already made when he'd knocked her out in the street. Pain had cascaded through her but she'd only given in when he'd told her viciously that he was prepared to send a video of him beating her up to her brother if that was what it took.

It had been the only thing he could have said to persuade her. Saul must never know what had happened to her in that crypt.

And now, after an unknown number of days, someone else had returned to the crypt. Her jaw still ached, but that was the least of her worries.

Shuddering, she bent her attention to the person in her dungeon. It was a man; was he the man who had forced her to dramatise her own misery so that her brother Saul would know she was alive?

She lay still, trying to pick up with subliminal receptors some indication of his identity. Strangely, she felt, with a hidden, atavistic shrinking, a strong impression of power and intensity, and beneath that a controlled menace that made her shiver with terror.

The muffled sound of his voice again, low, oddly compelling even through the planks of her prison and the earplugs, sent quick panic flooding through her, humiliating, loathsome, unmanageable. She tried to breathe carefully, counting the seconds, but it didn't help.

He spoke once more; although the words were somewhat louder they were still distorted by the physical response of her body. Her first reaction had been to will him to go away, but she suddenly wondered whether he was a passer-by who had merely stumbled on her prison. If that was so, he wouldn't know she was in the box on the floor. He might be her only chance to get out of here.

Nevertheless, it took a real effort of will to move, and when she did she moaned soundlessly at the pain in her cramped muscles. Clenching her teeth, she lifted her hands and hit the manacles sharply against the top of the box, hoping that the noise would be enough to attract his attention.

Strung taut by fear and foreboding, she screamed into the gag as the lid came up silently, yet with a rush of air that hurt her skin and proclaimed a violent energy in the man who stood above her. Ever since she had been locked in this coffin she had been desperately trying to get free, rubbing her wrists raw against the unyielding metal of the handcuffs, yet now she shrank back because the impact of the stranger's personality—intense, lethal, forceful—hit her like a blow.

Danger, her instincts drummed; this man is dangerous! Some primal, buried intuition warned her that he was infinitely more of a threat to her than either of the men who had kidnapped her. She sensed an icy, implacable authority, a concentrated will that beat harshly down on her.

But when he spoke his voice was level, almost impersonal. 'Just lie still for a few seconds, Stephanie,' he said, his voice pitched to pierce the earplugs.

So he was no casual passer-by.

Stephanie made herself stay quiescent as the gag was removed. This man knew exactly what he was doing, and did it as though he'd been wrenching off gags all his life. Life pulsed through him, an intensity of vigour, of purpose, a sheer, consuming energy that bathed her in white-hot fire.

Get a grip on yourself, she commanded. He still might come from the kidnappers. She said rustily, 'Who are you?' and strained to hear his answer.

'I've come to take you out of this. How do you feel?'

Relief was a slow, reluctant warming. 'I'm all right. Just numb all over.'

'You'll hurt like hell when the feeling starts to come back,' he said.

Her kidnappers had left nothing to chance; they hadn't intended her to escape. When he felt the steel manacles on her wrists and ankles the unknown man cursed roughly, but his hands on her body were warm and deft and gentle, and after a bit of manipulation the steel fell loose.

Nevertheless, it seemed an aeon before she was out of her coffin. Her legs wouldn't support her, so her rescuer held her with an arm around her waist and then all she could think of was that she was filthy and naked and that she must smell and look disgusting. She put up a fleshless, quivering hand to remove the plugs from her ears.

'I'll do that,' he said. In a moment the echo of her pulses that had been her sole companion for so many anguished hours was replaced by a rush of silence.

She didn't have time to appreciate it, for the numbness that held her body in thrall was overwhelmed by an agony so intense, she thought she might faint from it. Biting her lips to hold back mortifying whimpers, she clung convulsively to his broad shoulders as returning sensation surged through her with accelerating agony.

'How long have I been here?' she mumbled, trying to keep her mind off the torment.

'Three days.'

Free from distortion, his voice was deep and infinitely disturbing, detached, yet threaded by an equivocal undertone. English, she noted automatically, although there was something else, some hint of another country's speech; not an accent, more an intonation, a slight inflexion...

He sounded as though he could have spent enough time in New Zealand or Australia to be affected by their special and particular way of speaking.

Giving it up as too hard, she set her jaw and forced her shaking legs to straighten, her knees to lock so that she could stand upright. Sweat stood out along her brow, settled with clammy persistence into her palms. When the torture receded a little she managed to mutter, 'I tried to get free, but I couldn't.'

'It's almost over, princess.' His arm around her shoulders tightened. For several minutes he continued to support her trembling body, until at last he asked brusquely, 'Can you walk? Here, you'd better get rid of this——' Hands touched the blindfold.

Jerking her head away, she said, 'No,' because it gave her some sort of protection from his gaze. Not even when she had been stripped naked to the lewd sound of one of the kidnapper's comments had she felt so exposed, so helpless.

'Yes,' he said relentlessly. 'We're not out of the woods yet—literally. I don't think the men who snatched you will come back today, but if they do while we're still here you need to be able to see, and this half-darkness will give your eyes time to get accustomed to the light.'

Ignoring her panted objections, he stripped the blindfold from her shaggy head. Obstinately, Stephanie kept her eyes closed. 'Have you got any water?' she asked, running her dry tongue around an even drier mouth. 'I'm so thirsty.'

'Don't drink too much. It will make you sick.'

A metal flask pressed against her lips, and the blessed cool thinness of water seeped across her tongue. She gulped greedily, making a quick, involuntary protest when he took it away.

'No,' he said laconically, 'you can have some more later.' At her small sound of displeasure he went on, 'If you have any more now you'll be retching before you've gone fifty yards. Trust me, I know.'

An odd note in his voice coaxed her eyes slightly open. The torchlight barely reached the dank stone walls of her prison, but in its golden glow she saw a big man, tall and well-built, with a dark, angular, forceful face.

Shock hit her like a blow, followed by a strange, compelling recognition, as though she had always known he was out there, waiting. She would never forget him, she thought dazedly. He had rescued her from hell, and until the day she died she'd remember his warrior's countenance, stark in the earthy dampness of her prison, as well as his curt, understated consideration.

'That's better,' he said bluntly. 'Put these on.'

He had brought clothes—jeans and a shirt in muted camouflage colours. Gratefully, she struggled a few moments with limp hands and weak wrists, before saying on a half-choked note of despair, 'I can't.'

Without impatience, he said, 'All right, stand still.'

Competent hands pulled the clothes on to her thin body; he even managed to fit a pair of black trainers on her feet. Although the garments felt amazingly good after the soaked blanket she'd been lying on, she knew that she wouldn't feel clean until she had washed herself free of this place.

In a hidden recess of her mind she wondered whether she would ever feel really clean again.

'Let's get out of here,' he said.

Nothing in his tone indicated a need for hurry, but Stephanie suddenly realised that the longer they stayed in the crypt, the more dangerous it was.

Compliantly she tried to follow him across to the door, but her feet refused to obey her will. She began to shake.

'I can't walk,' she said angrily.

'You'll have to.'

Although the words were completely unsympathetic, he grasped her hand in his lean, strong one, and somehow she could move once more. Each step felt like knives in her flesh. Abruptly the story of the little mermaid and the sacrifice she had made to gain a human soul flashed into Stephanie's mind. When her mother had read it to her she hadn't liked the tale, finding it too sad, but until that moment she hadn't understood what a truly awful torture Hans Christian Andersen had devised for his heroine.

Tightening her lips, she held back any expression of pain. But when her rescuer switched off the torch and the blackness pressed in again, she couldn't prevent a choked cry.

'If you can't keep quiet I'll have to gag you again,' he said, each word stark with the promise of retribution. 'Walk softly, and *don't talk*. If anything happens to me, climb a tree and stay there. Most people don't think to look upwards.'

The next second she was stumbling behind a man who moved without sound. The door swung open silently, letting in a flood of dim light. At first it hurt her eyes, but as she squinted tearfully she saw stone steps leading up to bars, and beyond them a forest of firs, their trunks and thick foliage blocking out the sun.

Closing the door behind them, her rescuer locked it before leading her carefully up the steps, his back to the wall, his head turned towards the entrance so that all she could see of his face was the stern line of jaw above a hint of square chin, the sweeping angle of cheek, the dark, conventionally cut hair. His hand still engulfed hers; although it was warm and insistent, she understood with a purely female recognition that it could be cruel.

At the top of the steps he waited so long that she began to drift into a kind of trance. Then, apparently satisfied that the woods held no lurking enemies, he unlocked the bars and slipped through, shielding her with the graceful bulk of his body.

It was like all the thrillers she had ever read—the gallant, aloof hero, the abused heroine, the dangerous trek to safety. Perhaps if she could have viewed the situation as popular fiction she'd have been able to cope with the sick dismay that washed through her when he turned up the mountain and began to climb, half pulling her along behind him.

Gasping within seconds, exhausted in minutes, she knew she had to keep going, so she gritted her teeth and ignored the pain. He helped, hauling her over rocks, stopping occasionally to let her regain her breath. Her heart was thumping too heavily in her chest for anything but its erratic beating to be heard, and in a very short time she was engulfed by a headache and a spreading nausea that almost subdued her.

But anything was better than being locked in a box, unable to free herself. With the characteristic doggedness that came as a surprise to most people, Stephanie scrambled behind her unknown rescuer, grateful for the trees that sheltered them.

At last the steep slope levelled out. 'Stay here,' he said in a quiet, almost soundless voice, pushing her unceremoniously into a crevice beneath a rock.

Stephanie collapsed, peering through the bushes that concealed the narrow cleft, but he disappeared before she had time to query him, so she put her head on her knees, stiffened her jaw to stop the shameful whimpering she could barely control, and let her body do whatever it needed to recover. She was still panting when he slid back through the whippy, leafy branches with as little fuss as an animal.

Still in the same low voice he asked, 'How are you feeling?'

'I've felt better,' she said quietly, avoiding the cold clarity of his gaze. 'On the other hand, just recently I've felt worse. I'll be all right. How much further?'

'About a mile.'

As she struggled out he said, 'I think it should be safe enough to carry you,' and in spite of her automatic recoil he picked her up and set off.

Keeping her face rigidly turned away, she wondered why liberty didn't taste as good as she'd imagined it would in those nightmare days of imprisonment. She should have been ecstatic, because she'd expected death, and now there was a future waiting for her. At the very least she should have been relieved. Instead, an icy chill eddied through her, robbing her of everything but a detached recognition that she had been imprisoned and was now free.

Freedom was easy to say, she thought with a scepticism that hurt. Common sense told her that her body would mend quickly enough, yet as she lay there in the powerful arms of the man who had released her she wondered whether some part of her mind would be incarcerated in that box for the rest of her life.

'My car's not too far away. When we get there I'm going to have to put you in the boot,' her rescuer told her, his voice reassuring but firm enough to forestall any protest. He still spoke as though they could be over-heard. 'It will be bloody uncomfortable, but it's necessary, and I've put a mattress in there to make it a bit easier. I'm almost certain no one's been watching me, but we'll be going through several villages and the last thing we want is someone remembering that I had a passenger. So you'll have to stay hidden.'

Although her skin crawled at the thought of further confinement, Stephanie understood the need for caution. Mastering the flash of panic, she said, 'Yes, all right.' She thought his words over before asking slowly, 'Will S—will my brother be there?'

'No.' He paused before explaining, 'He's busy dealing with the men who did this to you. You and I will have to lie low for a while until it's over. I can't even get a doctor for you in case they have a local contact, but I have some experience in this sort of thing.'

'I'll be fine,' she said automatically, wondering where he'd gained this experience. First-aid training? A book on how to look after kidnappees?

Being rescued, she decided, closing her eyes, must have addled her brain.

He climbed for what seemed ages. Mostly Stephanie lay in a kind of stupor, accepting without thought the novelty of being carried, the controlled, purposeful toughness of the man. It did occur to her that he must be immensely strong, for he moved without any visible signs of exhaustion. And although he might not think there was anyone watching she could feel his alertness, a fierce concentration on every signal sent by the world around them. Several times he stopped and listened.

Whenever that happened she made herself still and quiet, trying to slow her heartbeat, calm her racing pulses and the rattle of air in her lungs, the interminable thud and throb of her headache. Although she too listened hard she could hear nothing but the sounds of the forest—an occasional bird, the soft rustling of a breeze in the trees.

Once she roused herself to whisper, 'Are we there?'

'Not quite.' When he went to put her down he surprised herself by clinging. 'It's all right,' he said gently. 'I'm just going to scout around and make sure no one is about.'

'Don't leave me.' Although she despised the note of panic in her voice, she couldn't control it.

'I'll be keeping a good eye on you.'

A small, childish noise escaped her lips.

'That's enough,' he said sternly, bending to thrust her into a cleft beneath a rock that broke through the bushes. 'I haven't gone to all this trouble to lose you now. Just sit there, princess, and I'll be here again before you've had time to get lonely.' He stepped behind a tree and disappeared, far too silently for a man of his size.

Disgusted by her feebleness, Stephanie waited, wishing she could point her ears like an animal to get a better fix on his whereabouts. A tangle of summer-green leaves hid her from any stray passer-by, but not, she knew, from a determined searcher. Her rescuer's familiarity with this mountain slope surely meant that he had spent some time reconnoitring.

Fighting exhaustion, she peered past the leaves, trying to identify a glimmering patch of white that danced in the sun beyond a belt of trees. At first she thought it was a waterfall, but by narrowing her eyes she could see that it was too regular for that. Slowly, it coalesced into stone, a waterfall of stone—no, columns of stone.

There, some hundreds of yards away through the trees, was what looked to be a temple, chastely, classically Greek. Her eyes blurred; she blinked to clear them, but a cloud had passed over the sun, and the tantalising streak of white was gone.

Perhaps it had been a hallucination.

His return startled her. It was uncanny; he seemed to rise out of the ground like a primeval huntsman, so at one with his surroundings that the trees sheltered him in their embrace.

'Not a soul in sight,' he said. 'Let's go.'

His arms around her were intensely comforting, like coming home. Sighing, Stephanie leaned her head against his shoulder. He smelt slightly sweaty, so it wasn't as easy carrying her as he made it seem. Another scent teased her nostrils, faint but ever present, evocative, with a hint of salt and musk. Masculinity, she decided dreamily.

She knew that she must smell hideous, reek with the stale odour of confinement. A pursuer, she thought with a wry twist of her lips, wouldn't need to search for her; all he'd have to do was follow his nose to find her.

She was still wondering why this seemed so especially unbearable when he said, 'Right, here we are.'

However, he didn't go immediately to the car that waited in the heavy shade of a conifer. It wasn't hidden, but few people would notice it, for it was painted a green that blended with the long needles of the trees.

Just inside the confines of the wood he put her against the trunk of a tree, and stood blocking her from anyone who might be watching, his whole being concentrated on a hawk-eyed, icily patient scrutiny of every tree, every blade of grass, and the big, dark car.

When at last he did move it was with a speed that shocked her. Within seconds she was deposited on the mattress in the boot, choking back a moan as he firmly closed the lid.

The engine sprang into life; with no delay the car drew away from the picnic spot and turned down the road.

Even on the mattress Stephanie was soon profoundly uncomfortable. Her bones seemed to have no fleshy covering to protect them; she ached all over, and she was shivering. She was also worrying. So great had her initial relief been that suspicion hadn't had room to take hold. Now, cramped like a parcel, trying to ignore the thumping of her head and the tremors that racked her, she began to recall things she had noticed but not questioned. Whoever her rescuer was, he had keys not only to the crypt and the coffin, but also to the handcuffs that had manacled her in the coffin.

Saul, her brother, had an excellent security department, but it was highly unlikely that even the most skilled operative would have been able to get those keys. So unlikely that she had better stop believing that the man driving the BMW had anything to do with Saul.

Her quick, instinctive stab of revulsion warned her that she was halfway into the Stockholm syndrome—falling in with the wishes of her captor.

Think, she adjured her pounding brain. Think, damn it!

There had been no indication that she was a target; if her intensely protective brother had heard the slightest hint that she was in danger, he wouldn't have let her come to Switzerland without a bodyguard. Or with one, for that matter. The close relatives of billionaires were sometimes at risk; she had long ago accepted the constraints of her world, and co-operated, so Saul had no reason to keep her in ignorance.

If Saul didn't know, if he hadn't been warned, then none of his agents would have been alerted. According to her rescuer, she'd been imprisoned for three days. She had no way of checking the accuracy of this, but if it was true, was that time enough for one of Saul's men to discover who the kidnappers were and get close enough to them to be able to copy the keys?

It didn't seem likely, unless the kidnappers had left clues the size of houses. And somehow she doubted that; they had been frighteningly efficient.

It seemed important to know exactly how many keys there were. Even understanding that it was a mechanism to push the truth away didn't stop her from counting them: the keys to the box, then to the handcuffs, keys to both doors. Four sets of keys. And he had them all.

She dragged a deep breath into her lungs. All right, don't panic! What sort of person was he, this man who had walked into her life?

Although she hadn't looked at him carefully, so she couldn't recall the colour of his eyes or even his colouring beyond the fact that he was dark, that first swift glance had seared his features into her brain: a blade of a nose, high, arrogant cheekbones, eyes that had something strange about them. Did he look like a criminal?

Not, she thought bitterly, that looks were any indication. The man whose face she had seen under his torn Balaclava hadn't looked like a criminal. If he'd been any type at all, it was a small-time shopkeeper.

Whatever, until she knew for certain, it would be much safer to work on the assumption that either her rescuer was one of the kidnappers who wanted all of the ransom, not merely a share of it, or an associate who knew what they had done, was trusted by them, and had decided to cut himself a piece of the pie. That would explain why he was being so careful not to be seen by the original kidnappers.

It sounds, she thought feverishly, like the instructions in an Elizabethan play: *Enter first kidnapper with gag, blindfold and coffin, exit first kidnapper. Almost immediately enter second kidnapper, a large, athletic man with keys and strong arms.*

If that was so, she was in just as much danger as before. He could quite easily plan to keep her safe as long as Saul demanded reassurance that she was alive, then kill her when the money had been paid over.

Her heart skittered into a rapid cacophony while her brain veered off towards the messy heights of hysteria.

Calm down. Panic isn't going to get you anywhere.

With an effort of will that made her teeth chatter she began to breathe slowly, regularly, forcing herself to count the seconds. Eventually the churning flood of fear in her stomach subsided, and with it her inability to think.

Paradoxically, the only thing that comforted her was that he'd used the keys quite openly. If she'd been less of a cynic she might take that to mean he was legitimate.

Of course, he could well be devious enough to use them deliberately so that she'd be confused into accepting him as completely above-board. It wouldn't be the first time someone had imagined that because her brother was one of the richest men in the world Stephanie Jerrard was incapable of logical thought, with nothing but clothes and jewellery and gossip in her mind.

He could have fallen into that trap. However, in the few moments she had spent talking to him she had gained the impression of a keen, razor-sharp intelligence, the sort of mind that didn't make obvious mistakes. Apart from the keys, what else was there to base suspicion on?

The tension clamping her muscles began to ebb as she realised how little there was. He'd been evasive when she'd asked about Saul. Or had he?

Questions jostled around her aching head, forcing their way through to her conscious mind, battering her precarious self-control. How long was this journey going to take? She felt as though she'd been in the car for hours. Although they were now climbing quite steeply she couldn't smell any exhaust fumes. Perhaps when you travelled in the boot of a car you left the fumes behind. No, she told herself, don't get side-tracked. Think!

While the car twisted and turned smoothly around corners, she decided to do nothing. Her suspicions could be entirely wrong, and anyway, common sense told her she wasn't going to be able to do any running or hiding until she'd regained some strength. The two men who had kidnapped her were around somewhere, and if she ran away and they caught up with her again, she thought with a shudder, they might kill her outright. After all, she could identify one of them.

So she'd eat and rest, and she'd probe as subtly as she could. If her rescuer was a villain she might be safe while she pretended to take him at face value.

Of course, there might be a perfectly logical explanation for those keys. All she had to do was ask. And if she didn't like the answer, she could fake belief until she found an opportunity to get away from him.

As the car slid to halt, she froze. Striving to look weak and pathetic and entirely brainless, she coerced her muscles into looseness, wondering despairingly whether she should try to get away now, when he would be least likely to expect it.

Before she had time to make up her mind the lock on the boot clicked. 'We're here,' he said, reaching in and gathering her up.

She said raggedly, 'Where's here? And what happens now?'

'This is where we're staying.'

'It looks old,' she said inanely.

'Not very. It was built last century.' He set off for a door across the garage.

Frowning, she looked around. 'It doesn't look like the stables.'

'It's not. This is the old laundry, which was converted into a garage some time in the thirties.'

Apparently he wasn't given to fulsome explanations. She said stubbornly, 'What's going to happen now?'

'I'm going to carry you upstairs, where you can shower and go to bed. Then you eat, and after that you sleep.'

It should have sounded wonderful but the greyness she had fought so long and vehemently had finally caught up with her. Blankly she said beneath her breath, 'Thank you.'

Some emotion sawed through him, but his voice was steady and deliberate as he said, 'It's nothing. Think of me as your doctor.'

Her doctor was forty, a married woman wearing her sophistication with cheerful cynicism and an understanding heart. Stephanie smiled wearily.

'Shower first,' he said. 'I'll have to stay with you, I'm afraid, in case you fall.'

A week ago she would have refused point-blank, but it didn't matter now. She didn't think she would ever be modest again.

She forced herself to look around as he carried her across a high, mock-Gothic hall and up some narrow stairs.

'This looks like a castle,' she said.

'Seen plenty of them, have you, princess?' His voice was dry.

'A few,' she admitted. It couldn't hurt. He knew who she was. What he might not know, she thought vengefully, was how formidable Saul was. On the first suitable occasion she'd make sure he learnt.

However, not even Saul was invincible, and she'd have to try to get herself out of this situation. So, she decided with an odd lurch in her heartbeat, she had better take a good look at the man who might well be her greatest obstacle. Fractionally turning her head, she sent a sideways glance through her lashes.

He wasn't handsome, but strength and a compelling and concentrated authority marked the slashing lines of his face. Not a man you would forget, she thought, wishing her head didn't ache so much that she couldn't think clearly. Surely kidnappers didn't look as though they strode through the world forcing it to accept them on their own terms? The two who had snatched her certainly hadn't. The one she'd seen was short and thin, inconspicuous except for his flat, emotionless black eyes, and the other had behaved with all the flashy arrogance of a small-time criminal.

This man couldn't have been taken for a small-time anything.

Stephanie felt physically ill; her whole body was screaming with pain, she was tired and hungry and frantic with thirst, and in spite of her efforts to keep a calm head she was terrified with the sort of fear that only needed a touch to spill into panic, yet her first reaction to eyes where the light splintered into scintillating

energy was a sensation of something heated and unmanageable racing through her with the force of a
stampede. Some hitherto inviolate part of her shattered
in a subtle breaching of barricades that left her raw and
undefended.

Eyes locked on to his face, she was thinking dazedly,
What's happening to me? when the corners of that
ruthless, equivocal mouth tilted a fraction. 'Do you think
you'd recognise me again?' he asked, his tone imbuing
the words with a hidden meaning.

'I'm sure of it.' Self-protection impelled her to add,
'I believe it's a well-known syndrome; people do tend to
remember those who rescue them from durance vile. Incidentally, how did you get into that cellar?'

He shouldered through a small door off a landing at
the top of the stairs, walked across a room dimmed by
heavy curtains, through another door, and stood her on
her feet, turning her at the same time so that she had
her back to him.

They were in a bathroom, neat, white, with a start-
lingly luxurious shower, all glass and modern fittings.
As his hands supported her for the first agonising moments, he said calmly, 'It's not a cellar, it's a fake crypt.
The locks on the doors are not brand-new, and the men
who put you there didn't bother to change them. Your
brother wields a lot of power, and it didn't take long for
me to get a complete set of skeleton keys.'

'And the handcuffs?'

His mouth tightened, but his eyes held hers steadily
as he said, 'There are techniques for picking them.'

Stephanie almost sagged with relief, her reassured
brain spinning into dizziness. Of course; she had read
of skeleton keys often enough; she should have thought
of them herself. And hadn't Saul's chief of security told
her once that there was no lock invented that couldn't
be picked, given time, equipment and a deft hand?

Before she had time to say the incautious words that
came tumbling to her lips, the man who had rescued her

began to strip her as efficiently and swiftly as he had dressed her.

'No,' she muttered, trying to stop his hands.

'You can't do it yourself.' He unzipped the jeans and pushed them down around her hips.

He was right, but in spite of her previous conviction about her lack of modesty she actually felt intense embarrassment. She had her back to him, but there was a mirror, and for a breathless second she saw their reflections, her pale, thin, hollow-eyed face beneath a wild tangle of rusty curls, the swift movements of his long-fingered hands unbuttoning her shirt.

Hastily she looked away, confusion and shame battling for supremacy. Although he was gentle, those tanned fingers branded her skin, leaving it hot and tender, connected by shimmering, glittering wires to her spine and the pit of her stomach. A lazy, coiled heat stirred there, as though his touch summoned something forbidden but irresistible.

Stephanie bit her lip, trying to use pain to drown out those other, treacherous sensations. It didn't work, and in the end she gave in, her eyes caught and held by the strange power of his.

'You have eyes like cornflowers,' he astounded her by saying. 'That brilliant, rare, clear sapphire. It must be a Jerrard trait.'

So he had met Saul. Stephanie's suspicions fell from her like an ugly, discarded shroud. Bewitched by the new and unusual responses of her body, pulses jumping, she waited until he moved away to turn on the shower before shrugging off the shirt and stepping out of her jeans. A quick flick of her wrist hooked a towel from the rail to wrap around herself.

She stumbled, and he caught her, pulling her against the solid length of his body. Stephanie flinched, that insidious, unwanted awareness reinforced by his nearness. Although she was tall and not slightly built, against him she felt tiny, delicately fragile, an experience intensified by the unexpected burgeoning of a languorous femininity.

Her rescuer's austere face was intent as he juggled with the shower controls, but that concentrated attention was not bent on her; he showed no signs of a reciprocal response.

You're mad, she told herself as steam began to fill the shower stall. Look in the mirror—your bones stick out, you're filthy, and you smell. The sort of first impression no one ever overcomes. Who in their right mind would be anything but casual and very, very detached?

'There, that should be right,' he said, urging her into the big, tiled, warm shower with its glass doors now tactfully obscured by steam. He didn't move away from the door, but at least he couldn't see much through the hazy mist.

A singing, surging relief persuaded her to release the bonds of the obstinacy that had held her together for so long. Only for a few hours, she thought as with eyes tightly shut she tried to wash herself. She could give up for a few hours and use some of this man's strength until she regained her own.

The water was like nectar over her skin, but its heat drained her waning energy, and her hands shook so much that she couldn't get soap on to the flannel. As tears squeezed their way beneath her lashes she continued grimly on, aware of the man who stood so close, a large, dim figure through the glass doors.

The cake of soap plummeted between her fingers and landed on her foot. Unable to prevent a soft cry of pain, she cut it short and crouched to pick up the wretched thing. It took a vast effort to push herself upright, and when she got there she could feel her legs trembling. Refusing to look at the man who watched, hating him for not leaving her alone, she gripped the flannel and passed it over the cake of soap.

He asked tonelessly, 'Do you want me to wash you?'

Lethargy enmeshed her, but she said, 'No, I can do it.'

Only she couldn't. Her arms ached, and her fingers wouldn't obey her, and her legs felt as though the bones had been replaced by sponge rubber.

He waited until she dropped the soap again, then said curtly, 'Here, give me that flannel. When you've as much strength as a cooked noodle courage and determination will only get you so far.'

Stephanie turned her face away, saying stiffly, 'I'm all right——'

'Shut up,' he said, interrupting her by taking the cloth from her lax fingers.

CHAPTER TWO

HOSTILITY flared brightly inside Stephanie, matched by a crackle of antagonism from him. A searing glance from those colourless eyes warned her that she wasn't going to win this one. Squeezing her eyelids shut, she stood mutinously while the flannel slipped slowly, gently over skin that was stretched and too sensitive.

Her blood gathered thickly in her veins. No matter how much she tried to concentrate on relief at being safe, all she could feel was the elemental nearness of the man who had brought her out of hell. His presence was a sensuous abrasion on her skin, electric, tingling, charging the shower stall with a fierce, primal vitality, setting acutely responsive nerves alight. Dazed, she set herself to endure what she couldn't change.

He didn't hurry. The flannel laved her body in subtle, diligent torture. He even shampooed her hair, working suds through the rust-coloured strands, seeming to understand that she needed it rinsed over and over until it was glowing against her head. Luxuriating in the purifying spray of water, she thought that he was surprisingly patient. She suspected that it wasn't an inherent part of his character, but had been hard-won by the exercise of will. Whatever, she was grateful for it.

Sudden exhaustion robbed her bones of strength, and she swayed, her hands whipping up to grab his forearm as she fell. Unwillingly her eyes popped open. A wide, bare chest filled her vision, fine wet hair slicked in a tree-of-life pattern over olive skin clearly in the best of health, a shocking contrast to her own sunless pallor.

Without her volition her gaze travelled down; she realised he still had his trousers on.

'You're getting wet,' she said foolishly, trying to curb a harsh, unbidden response, elemental and unwanted.

'I didn't think you'd like it if I came in without any clothes on,' he returned, a satirical note edging his tone.

Blood stung her cheeks and throat. Feeling much younger than her eighteen years, she stammered, 'No—well, no, I wouldn't.'

She had wanted to stay beneath the water until her skin was wrinkled and pale, washing off the results of being locked in a coffin for three days, scrubbing herself free from the taint and the terror and the evilness of it. But now she needed to get out of there.

Quickly, she said the first words that came into her head. 'I'm cold.'

'All right.' He turned off the spray.

Swallowing a lump that obstructed her throat, and apparently her thought processes too, Stephanie watched through lashes beaded with drops of water as he pushed open the glass door and stepped out on to the mat. Muscles moved in his back—not the smooth, sculptured works of art nurtured in a gym, but tautly corded, with the flowing vigour and hard, tensile power of rigorous work.

'Here,' he said, handing her a large, warm white towel.

Battling the treacherous feelings that surged through her, she accepted it and began to dry herself. He pulled another towel from the holder and started to wipe the glistening water from his arms.

Her last vestiges of energy evaporated as fast as the water on his skin. Stumbling once more, Stephanie would have fallen if he hadn't sensed her predicament and whirled around to catch her, moving with a speed and accuracy that obscurely frightened her. For the second time in as many minutes, she was supported against a taut male body.

'My legs won't hold me up,' she muttered, unable now to hide her panic with anger. Sensation bludgeoned her; acutely aware of the heated, silky dampness of his skin,

the potency barely leashed in the tall body that supported her, she swallowed.

'Stand still,' he said in a cool, crisp voice, and began
to blot the water from her shoulders.

Beneath the white towel his hands were careful yet
completely impersonal. By the time she was dry
Stephanie was shivering, engulfed by a fatigue that was
only partly caused by her ordeal. Dimly she realised that
she was being put into a huge T-shirt, thick and soft and
enveloping, before being lifted and carried and lowered
into a bed, and then sheets were pulled over her and she
sank gratefully into the sleep that claimed her...

Until the nightmares came like evil wraiths, tor-
menting with the terrors she hadn't allowed herself to
feel while imprisoned, slyly sneaking through the un-
guarded gates of her unconscious mind and into her
brain, vivid, horrifying, so real that she could feel herself
screaming.

'Stop that right now,' a masculine voice ordered,
compounding her fear.

A reflex action filled her lungs with air. Opening her
mouth to scream again, she flung herself on to the other
side of the bed. The sound was cut off instantly by a
hand clamping across her mouth. Bucking with terror,
she lashed her tired limbs to greater efforts, wrenching
at iron fingers, trying to bite, to claw, to scratch.

'Stop it, you little spitfire,' he commanded.

It was the impact of his body rather than his voice,
low and gritty and threatening, that restored her to her
senses. Suddenly she realised where she was, and that
this man had taken her from darkness and horror and
cleaned her and soothed her, as well as giving her water
several times already that night when she'd woken
gasping for it.

A convulsive shudder shook her and she stopped
fighting. Amid the fading panic and confusion she registered the change in his tone as he repeated, 'Stop it,

Stephanie. You're safe, and no one is going to hurt you again.'

Silenced, the only sound the heavy pounding of her heart, she nodded feebly. The hand across her mouth gentled, relaxed, and slid down to the pulse that beat ferociously in her throat. 'Poor little scrap,' he said, his deep voice vibrating with a barely curbed anger.

Somehow the simple remark called her back from the frightening world of her memories. She didn't want to be pitied, pity weakened her, yet for a moment she let her craving for security pacify her back into childishness.

'I'm sorry,' she whispered. 'It was just a dream.'

Perhaps because that long walk in his arms had desensitised her, or perhaps because of his total lack of response to her nakedness in the shower, she forgot any reservations she had and followed her simple need for reassurance by burrowing into him. As his arms tightened her panic eased into a strange contentment. She pressed her cheek against a bare chest, the slight roughening of his hair on her skin a profoundly comforting sensation.

He moved, but only to switch on a small bedside lamp. The light and his heat and solidity eased the chattering of her teeth, reached through her defences in some subliminal way and soothed her, as did the quiet rumble of his voice reverberating from his chest to her ear.

'You're safe,' he said again. 'No one will hurt you here.'

She could remember her father holding her and saying the same words. He had been proved wrong, and she knew that the man who held her so sweetly couldn't guarantee his words either, but for the moment she allowed herself to believe him. Tiredness and the heart-warming feeling of being sheltered and protected combined to make her yawn.

'I'm sorry I'm such a wimp,' she said in a slurred voice when she could speak again.

'You're allowed a couple of episodes. Go back to sleep,' he said. 'If the nightmare comes back, try telling it you won, you triumphed. But sometimes they're actually good for you, even though they scare the hell out of you. It's one way the brain can try to make sense of what happened.'

'I *know* what happened,' she said grimly, resisting the possibility of any more dreams.

'Oh, intellectually, but I'm willing to bet that in your heart you're wondering how anyone could be so cruel as to put you through the particular hell they organised for you.'

'Money. That's what it usually is. Some people will do anything for money.'

'You're very young to be a cynic.'

'I'm eighteen,' she said.

He gave a ghost of a laugh. 'And I'm twenty-five. I'm still considered young, so where does that leave you?'

'Childish,' she retorted almost on a snap, pulling free. The quick spurt of defiance exhausted her and his comment forced her to realise that he wasn't her father. He was a total stranger, and a rather frightening one, because beneath the feeling of safety engendered by those strong arms there were other emotions, deep and bewildering, that combined to produce the subtle, wild attraction calling to her with a honeyed, siren's voice.

Trying to speak without any indication of her runaway reactions in her tone, she said, 'I'm all right now, thank you. I'm sorry I woke you.'

'Princess, you didn't wake me.'

She huddled back under the warm duvet, averting her face so he couldn't see it. 'Why do you call me that?'

'Princess? That's what you are, isn't it? A genuine eighteen-carat-gold princess, with everything but the title. And your brother could probably buy one of those for you if you weren't too fussy about its origins.'

As she thought this over, wondering how an amused voice could be so detached, the mattress beside her sank, and to her appalled astonishment she felt the covers twitch. Sheer shock jackknifed her upright.

'What the hell are you *doing*?' she demanded in a high, shrill voice, staring with dilated eyes as he turned to look at her.

'I'm making myself comfortable,' he said mockingly, crystalline eyes gleaming. 'You can't expect to hog the covers, you know. It's bad manners.'

'You're not——'

He interrupted with unexpected curtness, 'Stephanie, you're quite safe. I'm *sleeping* here, that's all.'

'But what—then why——?'

He said reasonably, 'Although I'm almost certain no one is watching this place, I believe in caution, so I'm working on the assumption that we're under surveillance. The last thing we need is for anyone to realise that there are two people living here now. So we act like one person. We sleep together, we move around the house together; when you're in the bathroom, I'll be next door with the light out. I'm going to stick as close to you as a shadow, princess, closer than a lover, but I'm not going to touch you.'

When Stephanie gathered her wits enough to object, he didn't let her get more than a word out before finishing with a steely authority that silenced her, 'Rules of the house, princess; don't knock them—they might save your brother a lot of money and both of us quite a bit of trouble.'

The problem was that she understood. Having grown up in a small English village, she knew too well just what a hotbed of gossip such places were, and how by some osmosis everyone learned in an astonishingly short time all about everyone else.

But although his logic made sense, a wary feminine apprehension rejected it. The close, constant proximity he insisted on was going to be an enormous strain on her. She pulled the duvet around her body, trembling in spite of the mild temperature. 'No! I'll be very careful——'

'I'm not suggesting this, or giving you power of veto. You have no choice, so you'll avoid unnecessary stress if you just accept it.'

His voice remained cool, almost indifferent, but she heard the curbed irritation buried in the words as well as the implacable resolution. She gulped. 'I don't want to!'

'Stephanie, if you're afraid that I won't be able to control my lust, rest assured that I am not attracted to thin, gangly schoolgirls, even when they have indecent amounts of money as well as big, innocent cornflower eyes and a mouth as soft as roses.'

No contempt coloured his voice, nothing but that steady detachment, yet each word was a tiny whip scoring her skin, her heart, as it was intended to be.

She retorted obstinately, 'I'm not sleeping in this bed if you are.'

Unimpressed, he said, 'Then sleep on the floor; I don't give a damn. But just in case you're stupid enough to run around the house putting lights on, I'll tie you to the bed-leg first.'

Stephanie bit down on a gasp of outrage. Her gaze flew to his face; she read an implacable, unwavering purpose there. He meant every word. If she made up a bed for herself on the floor he would shackle her. At that moment, ensnared in the ice of his eyes, she hated him with every part of her soul.

However, two could play the game of threat and counterthreat. Her lips tightened. 'Saul won't like that.'

He directed a hard, level stare at her. 'Your brother will have to accept that I know what I'm doing.'

Flinging caution to the wind, she said rashly, 'He can ruin your career.'

As soon as she'd said the words she'd realised it wouldn't work, but she hadn't expected the deadly silence that followed. When he spoke his voice was slow and even and truly terrifying.

'Perhaps we'd better get one thing straight,' he said. 'I am not afraid of or intimidated by your brother. I never have been, and I don't plan to be in the future. In your world, princess, money might mean power. In mine it doesn't. Now lie down and shut up before I say something I might regret.'

More than anything in the world she needed to make some gesture, prove that he couldn't make her do what he wanted, but something in his stance, in the way his crystalline gaze met her rebellious eyes, something in the remote, chillingly indifferent face with its angular bone-structure and complete absence of softness or compassion, warned her not to try.

Defeated, she shuddered, almost swamped by the fear she had fought so valiantly. He was as callous as the kidnappers, finding the right buttons, pushing them relentlessly.

'Very well,' she said, striving for dignified self-possession, 'but using physical strength is just as despicable as using money to force anyone to do what you want them to.'

'I suppose it's your privileged upbringing,' he said conversationally, 'that means you don't know when to stop,' and before she realised what he was doing he caught her wrist in a grip just short of painful and leaned over and kissed her with a merciless mouth, crushing her objections, her worry and fear to nothing.

It was over in a moment. As she dragged painful air into her lungs, he stared at her with eyes as cold as shards of diamonds and said beneath his breath, 'God, what the hell are you doing to me?'

Stephanie's world had turned upside-down, been wrenched from its foundations by a kiss, as it had not been by the preceding nightmarish days. For a lifetime, for an aeon encompassed by the space between two heartbeats, she was captured by those eyes, dragged into a world where winter reigned supreme. This man, whoever he was, moved and breathed like a human being, but, in spite of his gentleness and care for her, at his heart was a core of primeval ice.

The prince of ice, she thought, trying to be flippant, an effort spoiled by foreboding.

'Turn over and get to sleep,' he ordered in that quiet, lethal voice.

Silently she turned her back on him and crawled beneath the covers, enveloped by the instant warmth of down. Tense and resistant, she huddled on the edge of the bed. Heat prickled across her skin, suffused every cell in her body. For the first time in her life she felt a tug of desire in her loins, a strange sensation in her breasts as though they were expanding.

Stop it, she adjured her unruly mind fiercely; stop it this minute. But she couldn't, until finally she fell back on a childhood remedy for unpleasant thoughts and strove to block out the images that danced behind her retinas with a concerted attack on the seven times table.

Out of the darkness he said, 'I'm sorry, that shouldn't have happened, and it won't be repeated. You needn't be afraid that I'll jump you again.'

She couldn't answer; touching her tongue to lips that were tender and dry, she wondered why his kiss should have had such an effect on her. Beyond the somewhat inexpert embraces of several boys not much older than she was, she had nothing to judge it by. Oh, she'd had crushes, but her brother's overwhelming masculinity made other men seem pale and ineffectual, and it had been difficult to let down the barriers of her mind and heart to anyone less compelling than Saul.

Also, her very protective brother made sure that she was kept well away from anyone who might view his younger sister as a tempting morsel. Consequently, most of her friends at school were far more experienced than she was.

Although their family had always been rich, and grown even richer under Saul's capable hands, he wasn't a member of the jet set. He despised people who didn't work, and because he was deeply in love with his wife he preferred to spend the time he had to spare with her and their children. Stephanie, too, loved being with the half-sister she had come to know so late in her childhood, and adored being a favourite aunt. Saul, she knew, kept a close eye on her friends, so although she had spent holidays with schoolfriends she had never gone anywhere except with people he had known and trusted.

Which meant, she thought, as she lay rigidly in the bed, that she was pretty naïve. If she'd been more sophisticated she wouldn't now be so overwhelmed by the powerful charisma of the man who lay beside her in the huge bed.

And perhaps she had been conditioned to look for that concentrated authority in a man; growing up with Saul had persuaded her that there could be kindness and love in a man of imperious character.

Exhaustion gripped her in unrelenting claws, but she couldn't sleep. Acutely aware of every tiny movement her rescuer made, of the length of his body next to hers, of the sound of his breathing, the tantalising, seductive heat of his body, her nerves sang like tightened bowstrings.

She didn't even know his name, and here she was sharing a bed with him!

Resentment simmered, encouraged because it blocked out the strange equivocal warmth seeping through her body. She despised men who thought their superior strength gave them the right to dominate.

And she hated the fact that he was able to sleep when she couldn't.

He'd probably shared a bed more times than she could count. Like Saul, who had been unmercifully pursued for as long as she could remember, the man who slept beside her possessed a smouldering sexuality that every woman would recognise. Squelching a mysterious pang, Stephanie lay longing for him to snore. It would demystify him, make him an ordinary man.

Of course he didn't. Eventually her muscles protested vigorously at being locked in stasis; giving in to them, she turned over on to her back, moving inch by careful inch in case she woke him. He didn't stir, but her change of position had brought her closer, and she scorched in the heat from his body. Surely all men weren't as hot as that? He certainly didn't have a fever, so perhaps he lived on a fiercer, more intense plane than other men.

Hastily, she turned back again.

'Stop thrashing about,' he commanded, his voice cool and slightly amused.

'Goodnight,' she muttered through clenched teeth.

Strangely enough, sleep reclaimed her then, but with it returned the dreams. Unable either to banish them or allow them to take her over completely, she fought back, and woke to find herself once more in his arms, that cruel hand clamped over her mouth again to cut off her screams.

At last, when it had happened three times, he said brusquely, 'Right, that's it. No, don't scuttle back to your side of the bed.' His arms tightened around her; one large hand pushed her head into the warm, hard muscles of his shoulder. 'Stay there,' he ordered.

'All right,' she said in the flat tone of exhaustion.

He pulled the duvet over them both. 'Now,' he said, his voice as level and unhurried as ever, 'let's see if we both can get some sleep.'

Her last thought was that he wasn't naked; she could feel some fine material beneath her hand as she cuddled against him, her body and mind immediately responding to his steady heartbeat.

Towards morning she woke, still in his arms, his body heat encompassing her, his scent in her nostrils, a masculine hand lying laxly along her thigh. At some time during the night she had climbed over him, and was now lying half on top, her leg between his, her arm underneath his other shoulder, using him as a mattress.

Overwhelmed by a demand she didn't fully recognise, a need she had never experienced, by the sheer, male power radiating from him even in sleep, she woke with her senses fully alert, her body in high gear. Unknown feelings tingled through her and before she realised where she was she felt his awakening, and the surge of awareness through his heated body, the swift compulsion of arousal that gripped him.

Stephanie might have been innocent but she wasn't stupid; she had read magazines and books, listened to some of her more worldly friends, and she knew that a man could be instantly ready for making love to any woman if she turned him on. She understood what was happening.

What she didn't understand and couldn't fight was her own reaction, the heady, draining weakness that had invaded her while she slept, making it impossible for her to retreat as prudence commanded. Anticipation coiled through her in sweet, seductive promise, drowning out common sense, washing away morals and logic and caution.

She had to get out of this immediately, scramble free and get on to her own side of the bed. But her muscles refused to obey her brain. Something world-shaking was making her heart race, drying her mouth, dampening her skin with an unexpected sheen.

He said harshly, 'Is this what you want?' And the hand that had been across her back found the full curve of her breast, cupping it, measuring its soft weight in slow, sensual appreciation.

Fire invaded her, robbing her of strength. An incredible sensation shot down her spine and into her loins; in answer she gave a tormented twist of her hips, seeking some as yet unknown response.

'How many men have you slept with?' he asked, that raw note in his voice abrading her nerves as savagely as his expert caress. 'You certainly know how to get what you want.'

She would have sobbed with desolation when his touch lifted if he hadn't slid his fingers down her back, exploring with lingering thoroughness the sharp bones of her hip and the amazingly sensitive hollow beneath it. She held her breath, and suddenly, fiercely, he clamped her hips down, pushing the newly awakened, violently sensitive portion of her anatomy against his growing hardness. Stephanie gasped, biting back a moan, unable to control the shudder that ran through her at the wild pressure.

And then she was almost flung across the bed, and he said in a voice that left her with no doubt about his feelings, 'Sorry, princess, I was paid to rescue you, not act as your gigolo.'

Humiliation burned deep into her soul; she had to swallow before she could retort thickly, 'I didn't—I woke up like that, damn you! And it was you who forced yourself into this bed.'

'Clearly a mistake,' he agreed contemptuously. 'But then, I didn't really know what I was dealing with. According to most reports, you're a sweet, innocent little schoolgirl.'

Sunk in frustration and shame, she lay with her eyes clamped tightly shut while he got out of the bed. However, after a moment she asked miserably, 'What are you doing?'

'Making a bed,' he said curtly.

Her lashes flew up. He hadn't put the light on, but the wintry pallor of early dawn was seeping through the heavy curtains, and she could see his outline, and the pile of clothes on the floor.

'No,' she said involuntarily.

'Yes,' he said, lowering himself to it. 'In another five years, perhaps, I might enjoy taking what you've got on offer. In the meantime, however, I'm going to have to say no, thanks. Nothing personal, princess—I'm a professional, and we like things to be nice and tidy.'

Which made her feel even worse.

*   *   *

When she woke it was morning, and the sun was shining in through the window with a hearty fervour that released something inside Stephanie. For the first time since she had been kidnapped she believed, not merely in her mind but in her heart, that there might be some future for her after all.

And then her eyes fell on the pillow beside her, and she stiffened, remembering. In one involuntary motion she sat up and looked at the floor where he had slept. The clothes were gone.

Heat flooded her skin; bitterly, angrily ashamed, she sank back against the pillow. How on earth had she let down her guard enough to climb all over him while she was asleep? And then, even when she was awake, to lie there and practically invite him to do whatever he wanted? No wonder he had been taken aback, although he needn't have been quite so brutal.

A self-derisory little smile curled her wide mouth. Perhaps he was afraid she'd make a nuisance of herself. If so, he'd certainly made sure his rejection was cruel enough to convince her never to fall into that trap again. If he still insisted on them sharing a bed, from now on, nightmares or not, she'd keep to her own side.

Forcing her mortification beneath the surface of her thoughts, she gazed around a room in the shape of a half-circle, its walls made of wooden panelling, its ceiling plaster. Both walls and furniture had been carefully carved by superb craftsmen to look medieval. Even the armchair was decorated by over-exuberant fretted wooden carving.

Yet wherever she looked she saw the icy scorn in her rescuer's expression as he rejected her.

She had to face it. And although shame still stained her cheeks she thought resentfully that he had had no right to be quite so—so scathing. There was *some* excuse for her behaviour. Surely after an experience like hers it was normal to crave the reassurance of human warmth, the comfort of arms around her, the momentary return to childhood when parents made everything better, even though from the age of four she had known that parents could die, that love was not enough to keep her safe, that the arms and soothing voice of a strong man were only temporary refuges.

Anyway, natural or not, a need for reassurance was a luxury she couldn't afford, especially if it led to situations like that of a few hours ago. Her fingers crept up to touch her trembling lips. For a moment she fancied she could feel his kiss on them. Very firmly, she banished the memory.

She shouldn't blame herself for what had happened in her sleep, but afterwards—well, that was a different story. If she had immediately climbed off him and made it obvious she wasn't trying to seduce him she wouldn't be feeling like this—embarrassed, ashamed, and with a forbidden fire in her blood that had to be outlawed. Instinct warned her that she was asking for heartbreak if she allowed herself to become even slightly dependent on the man who had rescued her.

Stephanie had learned the value of accepting her own emotions, and now she admitted that keeping her heart whole might be a little difficult. He had come to her like a prince on a charger, saving her from a hideous fate. She was entitled to spin a few fairy-stories about him; he was the stuff of fantasy, the dark hero, at once gentle and dangerous, kind and threatening, armoured in power and a fierce, unknowable authority.

But, tantalising though her fantasies might be, she couldn't afford to fall in love with him, for as well as the heart-stopping attributes of his strength there was that cool, impregnable self-sufficiency and a callousness that hurt. He might be only seven years older than she was, but what had happened to him in those years set a barrier between them.

He was a loner, a man who walked by himself. Prince of ice, she thought again.

She gazed around once more, searching for clues to the personality of the man who had brought her here. She found nothing. There was a dressing-table made of sombre, highly polished wood, on which was a tumbler with a collection of wild flowers. Stephanie wondered if the brilliant blue one was a gentian, then dismissed the query. Candace, her sister-in-law, would know; she was the expert on gardens and flowers.

But the little posy made a pleasant spot of colour, and in some odd way reassured her. Turning her head, she surveyed the other side of the room. The bedhead was against the straight wall that divided the room from the bathroom and the landing. The other walls stretched around her, enclosing and comforting, as though they were holding her in a protective embrace.

'It must be a tower room!' she said out loud, delighted, and flung the covers back.

Still stiff and sore, she staggered as renewed pain throbbed through her, but even so she was halfway to the window when she was caught and pulled back, whirled abruptly and held by a cruel grip on her shoulders, to meet the impassive, glittering eyes of her rescuer. Yesterday she had been too dazed to realise just how unusual they were, although she had registered their concentrated compulsion. Now, imprisoned as unequivocally by them as by his hands, she almost gasped. Instead of the warm, brilliantly clear sapphire she was used to seeing in the mirror, this man's eyes were so pale as to give an impression of translucence, with white flecks in the iris that made them look like splintered glass. Such was the intensity of those eyes that Stephanie's struggles stopped immediately. Her own widened, darkness swallowing up the colour; she shivered with some strange inner confusion.

'Don't go near the windows,' he said roughly.

The fragile moment of happiness shattering irrevocably, she nodded. Instantly, he let her go.

It was the most difficult thing she had ever done, but she managed to look fearlessly at him. He had freed her, slept with her, comforted her and finally held her, his strong arms and the solace of his presence banishing the nightmares. Then he had unfeelingly rejected what her innocent body had offered of its own volition.

Those powerful hands held her life and well-being. He could snuff both out as easily as he had pulled her away from the window.

He made her heart falter. Partly it was his amazing eyes, but they were merely the most arresting part of a truly formidable man. At five feet nine she was accustomed to looking many men in the eye, but he towered above her by at least six inches—possibly seven, she thought, gazing up into a face far more impressive than handsome. Slashing bone-structure formed the basis of features that reminded her of an eagle, the fiercely hooked nose and dominant, angular lines of jaw and cheekbones reinforcing an arrogant authority. His straight mouth warned of self-possession and fortitude, although she recognised something ambiguous about that mouth, a hint of sensuality in its sharply cut outline that set female nerves jangling at some hidden, primitive level.

From the top of his blue-black head to the soles of his feet he was all edged, confident masculinity, but it was a masculinity tight-leashed by an almost inhuman will.

'Who are you?' she blurted.

Apparently not in the least affected by her bold survey, he'd waited until she spoke. At her question his lashes drooped, and a smile, mockingly amused, curved his mouth.

'Duke,' he said laconically, and to her astonishment held out his hand.

Most men looked stupid with a hand held out, a hand that was ignored. This one didn't; completely relaxed, he merely waited. Once more Stephanie glimpsed a monumental, hard-headed patience that sent a cold shiver flicking down her spine as she reluctantly accepted his invitation. She had long fingers and a strong grip, but in his clasp her hand seemed small and white and powerless.

'You know who I am,' she said uncertainly.

'We haven't been introduced.'

Later she would wonder whether he had enough intuition to realise that this introduction was a wiping clean of all that had happened previously, and even before entertaining the idea would dismiss it. In spite of his care of her the preceding night he'd been more forceful than sensitive, and his abrupt rejection in the morning hadn't revealed any insight or empathy at all.

At that moment, however, saying her name, asserting an identity, was a reclaiming of something that the calculated inhumanity of her imprisonment had taken from her.

'Stephanie Jerrard,' she said, and her head came up. While they shook hands she asked, 'Just Duke?' and thought how strange it was that she had called him a prince, an ice-prince. He looked more like a prince than a duke, and yet the name suited his careless arrogance.

'That's all you need to know,' he said, an indifferent note in his voice warning her off.

As their hands fell away he ordered curtly, 'The windows look out over the valley, so the only people we have to worry about are ones with binoculars on the far side. Still, remember that if anyone does see you here word may reach the men who kidnapped you.'

At her involuntary shiver he nodded, pale eyes ranging her face. 'And if that happens we could lose not only the small men but those who gave the orders. Then there are your brother's negotiations; while you're thought to be safely stashed he's working from a position of power. If we can fool them into thinking that you're still their pawn, we're going to catch them all, including the ones who've kept their fingers clean.'

'I only saw two men. What makes you think there might be others?' she asked swiftly, striving to hide the sick panic that clutched her for an unnerving moment.

Broad shoulders lifted in a gesture oddly at variance with his poised, controlled persona. 'Rumours,' he said without expression, his eyes searching her face keenly. 'I need to know everything you can remember about the kidnapping.'

'Now?' she asked, realising that she was still in the thick T-shirt she'd worn as a nightgown. From the way it slid down over her shoulders it was one of his.

'Yes. It's important.'

She said, 'I want to go to the bathroom.'

'All right.' For all the world as though he was giving her permission!

When she came out of the quarter circle of bathroom he was waiting between her and the door on to the landing with the controlled watchfulness of a hunter at last sighting his prey.

'Get back into bed,' he said, and, when she hesitated, ordered curtly, 'Hurry up, it's chilly in here and you're still fragile.'

He was right; she was one vast ache, and her legs felt distinctly disinclined to hold her up. Nevertheless, she was getting heartily sick and tired of being ordered around. A glance at that eagle face, however, blocked any overt protest. Wordlessly, she climbed into the bed, covering her long, thin legs with a flick of the duvet. The T-shirt slipped; hastily, colour heating her skin, she hauled the soft material over her smooth bare shoulder.

Which was stupid, for he hadn't noticed. Those cold, pale eyes didn't move from her face.

'I was walking back to the chalet,' she said. 'There was nobody in the street; it was so still, so peaceful. I was looking at the stars and thinking I'd like a telescope, when they just appeared——'

'What were you doing in Switzerland?'

'Surely you know all about this?'

His expression didn't change. 'Just answer the questions, princess,' he said.

She said angrily, 'I was on holiday with friends, the Hastings. I went to school with Libby. They were going to stay for another couple of weeks, but I was leaving the next day to meet Saul at Frankfurt. We were going to fly to Fiji. Candace and the children are at Fala'isi, in the South Pacific, and the easiest way to get there is from Fiji. Anyway, the Hastings were called back to London; their son was in an accident, and was pretty sick, so I stayed on.'

'Why didn't you fly to be with your brother?'

Stephanie muttered defensively, 'Saul was there on business. I thought it would be fun to be free for a night.'

'What were you doing in a street in the village?'

She looked down at the sheet, watching the patterns her fingers made as they pleated it. 'I decided to have dinner in the inn,' she said. 'It's famous for its food, and the maid at the chalet suggested it. The Hastings took their cook with them; I thought the maid was going to cook, but she said she couldn't. It seemed perfectly safe.'

'Tell me about her.'

'The maid?'

He shrugged. 'Someone knew you were on the street.'

Duke was a skilled interrogator. Whenever she shook her head he asked the right questions to get her mind going again, and he was remorseless, prising information she hadn't even known she possessed from her with a combination of astuteness and unsparing, relentless pressure.

By the end of the session Stephanie's head was throbbing, but she had fully described the maid and what had happened to her on that street—and subsequently—with a clarity that astounded her.

Later, she realised that she was still not entirely sure that she trusted him, for somehow she had forgotten to tell him she'd seen the face of one of the kidnappers.

When at last he fell silent, his face impassive except for the slight drawing together of his dark brows, Stephanie yawned, her lashes drifting down.

'I thought they'd just leave me to die there.' She looked down at her wrists. Almost absently she finished, 'I couldn't believe it when one came back with food and water.'

He swore, words that shocked her, then looked at the raw chafing on her skin where she had struggled against the handcuffs. 'Is that why you tried to free yourself, even though you must have known you'd never make it?'

She said quietly, 'Yes. The will to survive is pretty strong. And if you don't try, you don't get anywhere.' Common sense told her that she shouldn't ask the next question, but she had to know. 'How did you find me? It was like a miracle.'

A smile, half cynical, wholly lacking in humour, touched that equivocal mouth. 'Luck,' he said laconically. 'Luck and gossip. But mostly luck. Your guardian angel has been working overtime for you, Stephanie Jerrard. Right, I'll get your breakfast. Today you stay in bed.'

She rebelled at that, but he was right—she was too exhausted even to want to get up. However, just to assert some sort of independence, the moment he was gone she disappeared into the pretty bathroom and turned on the shower. He reappeared as though he'd heard a shot, coming through the door like one of the avengers of old, his face dark and angry.

'What the hell do you think you're doing? I thought I told you,' he said between his teeth, 'that if you shower I stay in the next room?'

Her mouth hanging open, she stammered, 'I—I forgot.'

'Don't ever forget again,' he warned starkly, his voice leaving her in no doubt that he meant what he said. 'All right, go ahead. I'll make the bed.'

It was bliss; she made a ritual of it, from her hair to her toes, and then, even though boneless with fatigue, cleaned her teeth with the new brush and paste she found beside the basin until her gums bled.

But she was acutely conscious of the tall, intimidating man who waited for her next door.

CHAPTER THREE

STEPHANIE emerged wrapped in a towel.

Without speaking, Duke tossed another of his T-shirts to her, this one smelling of fresh air and sunlight.

'Thank you,' she said.

He gave her an unsmiling look and said, 'Stay in bed this time,' as he left the room.

Arrogant bastard, she thought angrily, waiting until he was halfway down the stairs before pulling it over her head. Surely he could have got her a nightgown?

'Here,' he said, appearing silently and far too quickly at the door with a tray which he must have had stashed on the landing. 'Breakfast.'

Oh, lord, had he seen her getting changed? Did he think she was trying to séduce him again? A swift, horrified glance from beneath her lashes revealed nothing but that inscrutable expression she was beginning to know so well.

Anyway, who was she fooling? The mirror in the bathroom wasn't very big, but it had revealed only too cruelly a gaunt face above a scrawny neck and hollowed shoulders, stick arms and blotchy skin. He might have been aroused in the semi-sleep of morning, but no man would want a woman who looked like her.

A forgotten nursery smell rose to her nostrils. 'Bread and milk!' she exclaimed. 'I haven't had that for years!'

The sense of smell worked its eerie magic. Somehow the simple, easy dish brought back an aura of those happy, protected days. Forgetting embarrassment, Stephanie smiled radiantly at him.

'Hop into bed,' he said shortly, and waited until she had obeyed before putting the tray on her lap. His closeness set off unfamiliar piercing sensations in the pit of her stomach.

As though he knew what he was doing to her he straightened and stood back, those glinting eyes cool and dismissive. 'You don't look much older than when you were in the nursery,' he commented. 'How are your wrists after that shower?'

It was another rejection, a reimposing of the boundaries he had set, and although a little kinder than his previous one it hurt. Pride aroused, Stephanie lifted her head in a queenly gesture. 'Much better, thanks,' she replied.

'Let me see.'

Reluctantly, she held out her hands. The steam from the bread and milk curled around the palms, dampening them.

'Turn them over,' he said crisply.

She obeyed, staring intently at the raw patches.

'You must be healthy, princess,' he said. 'There's no sign of infection, but I'll get you some aloe vera gel to help the healing. How about the rest of you?'

Her gaze flew up to meet his. 'I'm all right.'

Aloof eyes searched her face. 'Did they rape you?'

All warmth drained from her skin, leaving it clammy. She snatched her hands back and turned her head away so that he couldn't see her eyes. 'No,' she said harshly.

'I washed you,' he said without any change in his voice. 'I saw the bruises. I've seen marks like that before, and I know what they mean.'

'What sort of life have you *led*, for God's sake?'

He raised his brows. 'Mostly outside the palace walls,' he said indifferently. 'In places where innocent people quite often get hurt through no fault of their own. Places where virgins are raped and children killed before they've had a chance to live. Did they rape you?'

She hated him for not leaving it alone, hated him for making her face what had been done to her. But his stance and the unhurried resolution of his voice told her that she wasn't going to be let off. Normally she'd have died rather than tell anyone, but without too much of a struggle she surrendered to his stronger will.

'No. I was unconscious until just before they put me in the coffin. I woke up when they were taking my clothes off.' Banishing the memory of the jeering comments that had been the first sounds she had heard then, she said in a studied tone, crystal-clear, totally lacking any expression, 'One of them, not the one who brought me the food, wanted to. Rape me, I mean. He grabbed my legs and was forcing them apart when——' She stopped, remembering those horror-filled moments, her sheer, bewildered terror and useless struggling, then went on in a dispassionate voice, 'The other man wouldn't let him. He said it was wasting time; they'd been seen and they had to get out of there.'

Duke didn't say anything, didn't even move, but naked aggression, cold as the point of a sword, radiated from him. There was no doubt about it; the man who had rescued her was more than capable of killing.

'It could have been worse,' she said, trying to break the sudden, heavy tension with objectivity.

'The older one is a professional.' He spoke calmly, that wave of ferocity subdued by a determination so vast that she was frightened all over again. 'The younger one is a common, street-corner thug. Don't worry, they'll pay for what they did.'

'You know who they are?'

'Oh, yes.' It came as a chilling snarl, but when she looked up he seemed almost to be smiling. 'Yes, I know who they are.'

'How?'

'It's my business to know these things.'

'If you knew so much, why did you put me through all that—that interrogation?' she demanded, angry colour smouldering in her cheeks.

'To see whether you knew any more than I did,' he said unhurriedly. 'Eat your breakfast, and then you can sleep again.'

The quick flare of irritation had exhausted her. Hiding a yawn, she asked drowsily, 'Does Saul know that I'm all right?'

'Yes.' His voice was guarded. 'Don't worry about him.'

From beneath lowered lashes Stephanie watched him leave the room. Although her brother was a tall man, well-made, graceful, Duke was something else again, much bigger-boned than Saul, yet in spite of his size he shared the same noiseless ease of movement, an inherent air of great physical competence.

Sighing, she began to eat, but after several spoonfuls her hunger turned abruptly to near-nausea, and she abandoned the bread and milk. He had put a multi-vitamin tablet in a small dish; she used the diluted orange juice to wash it down, before putting the tray on to the bedside table. Then, as swiftly as a striking arrow, she went back to sleep.

For lunch he prepared delicious chicken soup and some toast, but later she suffered severe stomach cramps for an hour or so. Duke had apparently been expecting them and, while she endured the pain with as much fortitude as she could summon, he sat beside the bed and talked to her. They discussed books, the theatre, art, but nothing personal. His incisive mind, that of an intelligent, well-read man, made her feel inadequate and childish, a schoolgirl.

Which was obviously how he thought of her, if the bread and milk was any indication. A schoolgirl with a vigorous sex life.

That night she was sound asleep when he came to bed; at some time she woke and, drugged by the demands her mending body made of her, put out her hand to see whether he was there. Terrifyingly, the instant her fingertips grazed his hot, smooth skin he pinned her wrist to the bed beside his shoulder, his grip clamping the fragile bones in her wrist painfully together, numbing her hand.

'It's only me,' she whispered shakily.

'All right.' His voice was smooth and steady, with no sign of sleep in it. Releasing her, he asked, 'Did you have a nightmare?'

'No. I just wondered whether you were there.'

'I'm here.'

She couldn't discern anything in his voice, but it suddenly occurred to her that he might think she was making a pass at him.

Again.

Cradling her maltreated wrist, she turned her back to him and lay still, listening to his slow, even breathing. Had he been awake? He had responded with the deadly speed of a hungry animal; what experiences had given him the reflexes of a predator, swift, noiseless, lethal?

Experiences gained in that world outside the palace walls, she supposed, where the innocent suffered unjustly.

Eventually she fell into an unconsciousness punctuated by bouts of restlessness when her nerves jerked her back into the dark tower room with the man who was her rescuer yet a threat to her in ways she didn't yet fully understand. Each time she woke, she sensed that he woke with her, or so soon afterwards that he must have slept with every sense alert, honed to a razor-sharpness. But he never spoke, never made any movement, and she soon slid back into sleep.

That day set the pattern for the following one. Docile and lethargic, once more Stephanie spent ages in the shower and ate, her appetite increasing as she regained strength, but this time she insisted on getting up for lunch, and counted it a small victory when Duke agreed.

Of course, he laid down a set of conditions. 'You're not coming downstairs yet; keep well away from the windows, and you go back to bed after you've eaten.'

'What about some clothes?' Those eyes hadn't ever drifted below her face, but she was self-conscious about the length of thin leg that showed beneath the T-shirt.

'There aren't any, princess,' he said.

'There are. I wore jeans and a shirt——'

'I burned them.'

She stared at him. 'Why?' she asked stupidly.

'I don't want any but my clothes in the place. It's safer that way.'

Such concern seemed almost obsessive, and she said so, snapping the words out because an inner tension strung her nerves taut.

His mouth thinned. 'When it comes to my own safety I am obsessive,' he said brusquely. 'You can wear my dressing-gown.'

'No, it doesn't matter.' Ashamed of her shortness, she gave him an uncertain smile.

His expression didn't soften. 'It won't be for too long,' he said as he left the room.

She curled up in the armchair and stared longingly through the window at the alpine scene across the valley meadow and conifers, a small herd of cows, their cowbells clonking sonorously on the breeze, grass of an intense green. Bright flowers studded the grass, and insects would be humming through them, busy, mindless, their tiny lives measured by a season. Behind the summer-lit meadows and the darkness of the fir trees, the eternal mountains reached high into a cloudless sky.

Sniffing, she scrambled from the armchair and raced back to the bed, frantic to hide any trace of the tears that were gathering.

'What's the matter?'

Her head whipped around. Duke was standing in the arched stone doorway, those blazing eyes shrewd and speculative.

She shrugged. 'Nothing.'

He came in and sat down on the side of the bed, his gaze never leaving her face. 'Missing your brother?'

'Yes.'

His voice deepened, became hard to resist. 'And?'

She hesitated before muttering, 'I'm just being stupid. I'm free, I'm in reasonably good physical shape. I wasn't even raped. I should be relieved, and glad to be alive, and looking forward to the rest of my life...'

'But you're not.'

Without looking at him, she said, 'I just feel—grey. Not depressed, not—anything. I keep asking myself what there is for me, why I wanted to stay alive so much. Which is ridiculous.'

'It's only to be expected,' he said. 'You expended an enormous amount of energy keeping yourself together while you were imprisoned, so you're suffering from re-action now. Your body needs time to recover, but so do your mind and your emotions.'

She said dolefully, 'All I can produce is a kind of tepid pleasure at the thought of seeing Saul and Candace again. I feel as though I'm lost in a cold, foggy world where nothing really matters and where the sun is never going to shine again...'

To her shock and despair she found that she was crying, tears coursing down her cheeks in an unman-ageable flood while great gulping sobs shook her. Hor-rified, she turned her face into the pillow.

'Stephanie,' Duke said.

She tried desperately to stop, but his hand on her shoulder was the last straw.

'Don't try to hold back,' he said quietly. 'Crying is the best way of letting it all out. You've endured more than any kid your age should have to cope with, and you've come through it well. This is part of the healing. Let it go—you'll feel like a wet rag afterwards, but much better. Tears are not a sign of weakness; they heal.'

Surely it was uncommon for a man to understand so much? The thought wandered briefly into her mind before being driven out by the black flood of tears. Stephanie hadn't cried for years; she made up for it now.

When her final hiccups had died away she lay quiescent and motionless, Duke's handkerchief in one hand, her other swallowed by the warm clasp of his, and realised with a pang of dismay that she wanted to be in his arms. She thought caustically, Any man would do; you just want some sympathy, and knew she lied.

His voice was dry. 'I don't suppose you'll really rest properly until the men who did this to you are behind bars and you're back with your brother. Even then you might need therapy. You certainly need time. But don't be afraid; from now on I imagine your brother will make sure you're kept completely safe.'

Oddly enough, she felt perfectly safe now, with him. He was the one who insisted on the precautions.

He was silent for a few seconds, moments that hummed with unsaid words, undivulged thoughts and emotions. When he spoke again, it was on another subject. 'Tell me about yourself.'

'What do you want to know?'

'Well, what about your parents? Why is your brother your guardian?'

Somehow it didn't seem strange to tell him things she had never revealed before, not even to her best friend at school. Perhaps it was exhaustion, or the simple human need to communicate.

And perhaps, she thought, just before she embarked on the history of her life, it might be a good idea to tell him just how dangerous Saul could be when his family was hurt.

'I've had four parents, and lost them all. Careless of me, I've always felt. My father was the wild one of the Jerrard family, the one who never fitted in. He wandered out to New Zealand and found my mother. From all accounts he fell instantly in love with her.' Her mouth tucked in at the corners. 'It wasn't hard to do. Saul says she was fey, a beautiful, fragile thing like a bird with a broken wing. For those days, she was very wild. She'd already had another child before my father came on the scene.'

'You don't look like her,' he said. 'You're a Jerrard through and through.'

'I know.' With no trace of that mysterious sensuality that had impressed anyone who met her mother. She paused, looking down at the sheet. 'When I was four my father drowned and not long after that my mother committed suicide. My father's brother and his wife, Saul's parents, took me to England and adopted me. We were all very happy, but it didn't last. I thought they'd been killed in an accident, but a few years ago Saul told me what really happened.'

'Why?'

Trust him to home in on the uncomplimentary part of the story. She admitted, 'I was being stupid about security arrangements.'

'I see.'

There was an edge to his voice that puzzled her, but she said, 'I was at my most brattish then. I think I've grown out of it.'

'What happened to you after they were killed?'

'I missed them unbearably. Saul did his best, but he was extremely busy; when his father died my uncles thought that Saul was too young and untried to handle Jerrard's, and they decided it should be broken up so that each of them would own the part they were most interested in. Saul didn't agree, and there was a battle that turned vicious. I don't know all the ins and outs, but apparently it ended in a lot of bitterness. Saul was kept at full stretch for a couple of years tidying up the mess.'

'So you were left alone at your very expensive boarding-school.'

'If you can be alone with a couple of hundred other girls,' she said tartly. 'I knew he loved me. He was always there when I needed him, and he came to every sports day and prize-giving. Of course, we always spent the holidays together.'

'A nice, secure life. Are you jealous of his wife?'

Lifting her head, Stephanie stared at him with astonishment and anger. His ambiguous mouth was firmly disciplined, all thoughts hidden by the thick, straight fringe of his black lashes.

'I couldn't be jealous of Candace!' she said curtly. 'Apart from anything else, she's my half-sister.'

'Is she now?' he said.

It was impossible to tell whether he had known that before. He had a classic poker face, as unreadable as the sphynx, responses and emotions completely under his control.

'Yes. She was the daughter my mother had before she married my father, the child who was adopted out. Candace doesn't talk about her childhood, but I think it was happy enough until her parents' marriage broke up. Her adoptive father rejected her when his new wife had children, and her mother married a man who didn't want her. After that she lived in foster homes, but she was determined to find her birth family. By the time she was old enough to start our mother was dead, and Candace couldn't find out anything about her father, so when she tracked me down she wanted to establish contact. Luckily for me, she and Saul fell in love, so it all worked out very well.'

'Especially for Candace,' he said smoothly.

She sent him a very level look. 'Do you know her?'

'No,' he said.

'Then don't presume to judge. She and Saul are very happy together.'

His eyes narrowed further, but he said, 'I'm sure they are.'

'Who are you?' she asked abruptly, giving way to the curiosity that burned inside her. 'How did you find me? And don't give me that rubbish about luck and gossip.

I don't believe in luck, and no one gossips about a kidnapping.

'You'd be surprised what people talk about, and even more surprised at how much intelligence-gathering is just sifting gossip.' His mouth compressed as though her question had hidden ramifications. 'That's my job. I listen to gossip, and I find people.'

'Ah, an investigator.' She waited for him to agree but he said nothing, pale eyes watchful in an inscrutable face. After an awkward pause she asked, 'Do you work for Saul?'

'At the moment.' He got up to walk across to the window.

The hand he'd held felt cold, and Stephanie wondered why his touch had seemed to anchor her. Uneasily, she watched beneath lowered lids as he stretched, his wide shoulders and back flexing beneath the thin cotton of his shirt. Mysterious senses stirred, uncurled deep within her, turning her bones to liquid. She realised anew with a jolt of primal foreboding how very big he was, and how understatedly powerful.

Yet he could be gentle, as some really strong men were gentle. However, he wasn't giving anything away; he was treating her like a child, to be comforted and petted and fed and clothed, but not to be told anything.

Macho, masterful men, she decided indignantly, they were all the same; until Candace had come on the scene Saul had been like that. Candace wouldn't accept it from Saul, and because of her influence he had slowly allowed Stephanie a little more autonomy.

After this débâcle, she thought grimly, he was going to want to wrap her in cotton wool again.

'So how *did* you know where I was?' she asked, her voice lifting autocratically. Duke had evaded the question, and she was determined to make him divulge something.

The glowing light outside silhouetted his form in brilliance. Recalling that the Greek god Zeus had come to one of his lovers in a shower of gold, she wondered whether this was how the girl had seen him, dark body blocking out the light, surrounded by a fiery corona of sunlight.

He didn't answer until several seconds had passed. Then he moved away from the window and said calmly, 'I was called in because I'm the best at what I do, and because I'd passed certain rumours on to the men who work for your brother. Fortunately, when you were taken they contacted me immediately instead of waiting until the trail had gone cold. With the information I had, and what they'd managed to glean, we were able to work out who had kidnapped you; after that it was merely a matter of finding out what they'd done with you. Judicious questioning and tailing got me that. Then I got the keys and freed you.'

It all sounded so simple—far more simple than it had been, she was sure. A shiver pulled her skin tight. 'So you knew where I was from—when?'

'From when he went back to give you food,' he said, his tone revealing nothing.

It took a moment to sink in. Then she said incredulously, 'You mean you knew I was there—you let me lie there for a whole day before you came to get me?'

'Yeah,' he drawled, the word incongruous. 'That's exactly what I did.'

Although Stephanie had the temper that went with bronze hair and ivory skin, over the years she had learned that losing it gave others too much control of the situation. This time, however, as she searched the darkly arrogant face of the man who had rescued her, she could feel a familiar turbulence seethe through her, fierce and white-hot and irresistible. Each one of those hours spent in claustrophobic bondage, in filth and hunger and terror, would be imprinted on her memory for the rest of her life.

Her hand shook as she thrust it through the tangle of her hair, pushing it back from her hot face. Very evenly she said, 'I presume you had a good reason for leaving me there?'

'Oh, I did, princess, I did indeed.' His voice was hard and flat, without inflexion. 'I had to make sure that the two men—who are still in this area, and presumably were intending to visit you again—were out of the picture before I went anywhere near you.'

It made sense in a coldly practical way. 'And are they out of the picture?'

'They were then. Temporarily.' His mouth curved in a smile totally lacking in humour.

'Then why,' she demanded, 'all the elaborate secrecy? Why did we have to play cops and robbers all the way up the mountainside?'

'Because although I managed to send them off on a wild-goose chase I wasn't completely sure that they'd stay away for as long as I needed to get you out.'

Again his actions made sense, but—what sort of man was he, to leave her to the mercy of that crypt? He hadn't even known that she was all right. She could have died before he came.

Not for the first time in her life, although never before with such intensity, she faced the essential loneliness of humanity, the gulf that divided one person from another. He'd made a cruel decision, yet one fulminating glare at his face told her that he would do exactly the same thing again if he thought it necessary.

Prince of ice...

'How did you get them out of the way?' she asked, conceding defeat of a sort.

She could tell he didn't want to answer, see him choosing the right words. Finally he smiled again, an unpleasant twist of his lips that made her shiver. 'The less you know about it the better.'

She eyed him angrily, but it was obvious he wasn't going to tell her. Still, she tried. 'How much ransom did they ask?'

He shrugged, then sat down in the armchair, his face in shadow, long legs stretched out, watching her with unnervingly half-closed eyes. 'Twenty million pounds.'

Fighting the chill clamminess of her skin, she said quietly, 'Not even Saul could afford that much.'

Duke said, 'He's rumoured to be one of the richest men in the world, but that would be just a negotiating figure. They'd know he'd be desperate to get you back. You represent a lot of money, princess.'

Is that all I represent? she wondered forlornly. Just money? She had endured enough sycophantic behaviour at school to understand that many people valued her solely for the money her brother controlled, but something in her rebelled at being labelled a poor little rich girl. Damn it, she had things to offer the world, and it suddenly seemed important that she discover what they were, and use them. Then Duke wouldn't look at her with that kind of aloof pity, as though he too agreed with the men who had callously reduced her to a matter of pounds and pence.

Anger and pride and fear were ruthlessly subdued. Trying to speak objectively, she asked, 'Do they know I'm gone yet?'

'I don't know. I have to work on the assumption that they do.'

She cast a swift look at the window. They could be out there searching for her again. 'Then why can't I go home? Why do I have to stay here?'

'I told you. Your brother wants it.'

'He's keeping me out of the way, too,' she said with faint bitterness.

Duke's shoulders lifted. 'He's doing what he thinks is best,' he pointed out, a hint of impatience abrading his voice.

'Do you think he's right?'

His eyes met hers. 'It has nothing to do with me.' His voice was indifferent.

If holding her here was Saul's decision it would have been made with her best interests at heart.

Stephanie could understand her brother's reasoning. With her safely out of the way he had a much better chance of conducting his negotiations with the men who had organised her kidnapping. If she reappeared by his side they would simply go to ground, and possibly try again.

Unfortunately logic didn't ease the sore patch in her heart.

Duke got to his feet. 'Try to get some more sleep,' he advised. 'You spent last night tossing and turning.'

But not dreaming, thank God. Suddenly tired, she turned her head away from the golden glowing sunlight beyond the window. Just before unconsciousness claimed her she realised that while she had been imprisoned she hadn't dared sleep in case she didn't wake; now her body was catching up.

Quite late in the afternoon she woke, her bones lax and heavy, her mind floating free, oddly unconcerned, almost tranquil. For a while she lay peacefully gazing at the peaks, remote and icily silver as Duke's eyes, cutting their way into the tender blue of the sky.

When this was all over she would never again take sunlight and freedom for granted.

She got up and showered, then, rebelling at the inaction that had kept her in the tower, decided it was time she explored the rest of the house. But when she tried the handle on the door that led to the stairs she found that it refused to move.

She stood there, looking at the lock, a modern, completely efficient one, impossible to pick even if she knew how, while something like horror beat high and frantically in her throat.

Her shaking hand across her forehead momentarily smoothed out the puckers of fierce thought. She turned away from the door, then spun around and tried it again, rattling it in her frustration. It didn't budge.

Don't be silly, she told herself sternly as she went back to the bedroom. There's no need to make such a drama of a perfectly ordinary thing. Duke has probably gone to the nearest village for food and, not wanting to wake me, has simply made sure I can't go wandering around the place revealing myself to anyone who might be looking.

It was the sort of thing he would do.

She sat on the side of the bed, eyes fixed sightlessly on the scene through the window as the sun went down over the mountain, edging the sharp rim with gold, then fell into darkness. Dusk gathered itself against the steep slopes, thickened, merged into twilight and night.

Being locked in brought with it a temporary return of the terror she had fought so strongly in the crypt. She was still sitting on the bed, hands loosely clasped in her lap, when he appeared in the doorway. No footstep, no tell-tale click of the door warned her. Her heart sped up, the blood beating hectically through her veins, and for a moment she was held frozen by a bewildering confusion of emotions.

'Good girl; you had the sense not to turn a light on,' he said crisply as he strode across to close the curtains. 'I'm sorry I'm late back. I went down to the village and got waylaid.'

He reached past her and switched on the light. In the sudden blossom of radiance his face loomed, darkly intimidating and powerful, the crystalline eyes searching her face, dropping suddenly to the slender lines of her legs against the crimson coverlet, before flicking back up to her face. She could smell something warm and potent on his breath, and every nerve tightened, but it was obvious that whatever he'd been drinking hadn't been enough to affect him. She couldn't, she thought fleetingly, imagine him drunk. His impressive control would forbid such a weakness.

'They're celebrating their thousandth anniversary,' he went on easily, 'and everyone was enjoying themselves in the bar.'

'Do they know you?'

He shook his head. 'No; I only arrived the day before yesterday, after your brother organised the lease of the castle, but they're shouting free drinks to every passer-by. I don't want to cause any comment so I had a couple with them.'

'Why did you lock me in?'

Did he hesitate? No, although his gaze narrowed as he answered, 'Because I didn't want you wandering around where you might be seen.'

Those translucent eyes were hooded until he smiled. She wanted more of that smile, she craved it, and in that craving, she knew, was a danger more extreme than any other.

'And,' he added deliberately, 'to make sure no one found their way up here.'

It was like being dumped into polar water. A shiver worked its way across her skin. 'I don't like being locked up,' she said quietly.

'I can understand that. When I left you were sound asleep, and I intended to be back before you woke.' He wasn't apologising, or even making excuses. He was simply telling her, and somehow the deep, calm voice soothed her illogical fears away.

Nodding, she looked down at her hands, long and thin, somewhat paler than normal. How stupid she'd been, letting panic overcome common sense.

'Why did you try the door?' he asked.

'I wanted to look around,' she said without expression.

'Even though I told you that you are not to wander around the place?'

He was standing too close; he made her skin sensitive and prickly, sent strange little chills along nerve fibres she hadn't even known she possessed.

Feeling stupid and ungrateful, she said, 'I try to remember, but I'm not used to being a prisoner.'

When he spoke again his words were slightly more conciliatory, but his tone wasn't. 'Try harder. The last thing we want is to let anyone see you here.'

She nodded. 'I know. Believe me, I don't want to jeopardise things.' She looked at him directly. 'Are you in contact with Saul?'

'No,' he said instantly. 'He knows where we are, and he knows you're all right, but we decided it would be better to stay silent from now on.' He paused, then, clearly choosing his words, he continued, 'There's a chance—so remote that it's highly unlikely, but we have to take it into consideration—that someone close to him might be passing information to whoever kidnapped you.'

Indignantly, Stephanie said, 'No, I don't believe it.'

'Anything is possible, princess, especially when large amounts of money are involved, but I'll agree it doesn't seem likely.'

She gave a taut smile. 'And you are a cautious man.'

'It's not a fashionable quality, but it's saved my bacon too often for me to ignore it. You look tired. Get into bed and I'll bring dinner.'

'No,' she said quickly. Staying in bed had lowered her guard, setting up a spurious intimacy that gravely weakened her. She needed some distance between them, to put their relationship, such as it was, on a more normal basis. 'I'll help you get dinner,' she said, getting to her feet.

'Do you know how to cook?'

'Well, no,' she admitted.

'Peel potatoes?'

He was getting at her. She shrugged. 'It wasn't covered at school. But I'm tired of being stuck up here like an invalid, and this may well be an excellent chance to learn how to cook from a master.'

'Most bachelors are reasonable cooks,' he said, and her heart gave an odd little skip. He didn't expand on it, merely added, 'Who said hunger is the best sauce? I don't consider myself a master, merely competent, but thank you for the compliment. All right, you can come on down, but you sit at the table and the moment I decide you're tired you come upstairs again without any quibbling.'

She directed a mutinous stare at him.

'Otherwise,' he said, in a voice that told her he wasn't going to budge, 'you stay up here.'

She didn't have the strength at this time to fight him, so she capitulated, promising herself that one day he'd find out she had a will of her own. 'Did you bring me any clothes?' she asked, knowing the answer.

'No. You can wear my dressing-gown.'

'I'll *swim* in it.'

Brows raised, he surveyed the thin length of her body, too well revealed by his T-shirt. The colourless eyes gleamed, and something moved in them, something that sent Stephanie's pulse leaping into her throat.

Immediately he turned away. 'Wait a minute,' he said, striding across to the wardrobe. He opened the door and took out a shirt with long sleeves and tails. 'Here,' he said curtly, tossing it on to the bed. 'See how that goes.'

She almost ran into the bathroom, and for the first time locked the door behind her. The shirt reached halfway down her thighs. Rolling up the sleeves and fastening the buttons, she tried to convince herself that she was less exposed to him than if she'd been wearing shorts.

But there was a vast difference between wearing shorts and walking around with nothing on beneath his shirts, feeling material that had been against his skin caress hers...

A swift glance in the mirror told her that her eyes were glittering, the sapphire darkening to a brilliant cobalt, and her mouth looked soft and swollen and very red.

'Stop it,' she told the woman in the mirror, the woman with the fierce, turbulent expression. But that woman was busy remembering the glint in Duke's eyes as they'd followed a track from her neck to her breasts, full and high, and then down to her legs. She could feel the heat of his scrutiny on her skin now, burning into it, sending more of those messages to her nerves. For a few seconds he had forgotten that he'd been sent by her brother to rescue her, and there had been a virile male challenge in his gaze that had liquefied her bones. And instead of being upset or frightened or offended she had wanted to meet that challenge with one of her own; she had wanted to display herself, to preen in the light of his obvious appreciation, to show him that in spite of everything she was a woman...

She licked dry lips, trying hard to keep her brain cool and practical. Face facts, she told herself. You're scrawny, ill and unattractive; your skin and hair are both showing the results of several days without food and sunlight and freedom. And you're a girl whose only knowledge of the mysteries of men and women comes from hearsay and books.

So she had better just forget that occasionally Duke's masculine self overcame the prudence of his acute intelligence.

'Are you ready?' he asked from the other side of the door.

Jumping, she snatched up a face-flannel, ran the cold tap on to it, and held it for a moment to her heated face.

'I'm coming,' she said, and put it down before, with head held high and pulses skipping, she went through the door.

The castle, she found, wasn't very big. 'A Victorian whim,' Duke told her as they walked down the narrow, winding staircase. 'A crazy English aristocrat decided to build it here so he could botanise whenever he felt like it. Botany was the fashionable and romantic thing to do, and he was romantic to his heart's core. So he found a

suitable crag in the Alps and built this place. But that
wasn't enough. His wife decided it needed something
extra and persuaded him to add a couple of follies among
the fir trees.'

Stephanie smiled, imagining upright Victorian gentlemen sporting the usual amount of facial hair, and well-
bustled Victorian ladies with ringlets and coy eyelashes
and rosebud mouths.

Duke continued, 'It might look like a castle, but really
it's a holiday home, a bach.'

'Bach?'

He directed a long look towards her, a look she had
met with cool reserve, hoping very much that no sign
showed of the forbidden desires he aroused in her. The
only thing left to her was her dignity, and she was going
to cling to that for all she was worth.

'I suppose four years old is too young to remember
that in New Zealand's North Island a holiday home is
called a bach. In the South Island they call them cribs.'

'I didn't know that. Are you a New Zealander?'

'No,' he said abruptly. 'But I have connections there.
Have you been back?'

'Several times. I love it. So green and wild and fresh,
so—isolated and end-of-the-worldish. When we fly into
Auckland I'm always surprised to see a modern city
spread out below; the land and seascape look as though
the place should be something out of Tolkien, a haven.'

'A romantic idea.'

She reacted snappishly to his irony. 'Romantic no-
tions didn't go out with Victorian aristocrats. At eighteen
I'm allowed to be starry-eyed. In fact, I think it's almost
obligatory.'

'And here was I thinking you were a little cynic,' he
said, smiling, yet when she glanced sharply at him he
was studying her as though she were a rare insect to be
classified and tabled.

Something swift and keen moved in the pit of her
stomach, something akin to fear, giving an edge to the

response that still roiled through her. Careful, she thought as she went with him through the high hall with its suits of armour and dim battle-flags, through the green baize door that had separated the master from the servants, and into the kitchen. You must be careful.

CHAPTER FOUR

THE kitchen was a huge affair that didn't appear to have been altered much since the day it was built. A vast range of some sort was backed against a stone wall, purring gently to itself as it warmed the shadowy room.

'Right, you can have your first lesson in peeling potatoes,' Duke said.

Stephanie had always been deft, and the knife was finger-nicking sharp; nevertheless, ten minutes later she morosely transferred her gaze from thick peelings to marble-sized potatoes. When she got out of here, she thought, tipping the vegetables into the sink to wash them, one of the first things she'd do was take cooking lessons. This was ridiculous!

'By the time we leave here,' Duke said, turning from the bench in time to catch her dismayed expression, 'you'll be an expert.'

She laughed, hoping he didn't hear the jarring note. 'We're going to be here that long?'

'I assumed you were a fast learner.' Deftly, he continued doing things to steaks.

'I hope so,' she said, pretending to laugh again. 'Otherwise we're going to be bankrupted by constantly buying potatoes.'

'Not to worry, your brother's paying for them.'

'I hope you're buying them discreetly,' she said teasingly. 'It would be dreadful if, after all your care to make sure no one knows I'm here, someone deduced it because you keep buying potatoes.'

He sent her an unsmiling look. 'I brought most of the food with me,' he said. 'And don't worry, I'm being very careful.'

She sighed. 'If only we knew what was going on.'

72

'I know as little as you do,' he returned calmly, and, apparently not in the least put out by his lack of information, began to slice onions, the knife slashing through the white flesh with swift, sure movements.

Nodding, she thought with a flash of insight that it was an unusual role for him to play, the passive onlooker. Duke—if that was his real name—had all the hallmarks of a leader, not one who watched from the sidelines.

Nevertheless he didn't seem to be fretting at this enforced inactivity. He possessed a disturbing self-assurance, as forceful as it was seamless. In spite of her misgivings she wanted to know more about him, and she was prepared to bet that every woman who met him wanted the same thing. His particular brand of direct, uncompromising masculinity was an unconscious provocation to the opposite sex. She hadn't had all that much to do with men, but she'd seen women react to her brother, so she'd grown up knowing that there were some men who were almost irresistible to the opposite sex.

He looked up, catching her eyes. Hastily, she swished the potatoes in the water, snatching her thoughts away from such a hazardous premise.

Although she withstood the impact of his gaze on her face for as long as she could, pride eventually forced her to meet it. Apparently not at all concerned by the open defiance of her glower, he continued to examine her face in a slow, unwavering scrutiny, and to her embarrassment heat singed her cheekbones. She was accustomed to being looked at, but not like this, as though he was imprinting her face on his memory for all time.

'It's going to be all right,' he said quietly. 'A few more days here, and then you won't need to worry about this lot ever again.'

She shook her head, hesitating before putting her greatest fear into words. 'But there will be others,' she said eventually. 'Oh, not kidnappers, but there's always someone who wants something.'

'That's what happens when you're indecently rich,' he mocked, sardonic humour bracketing the sides of his straight mouth.

She said acidly, 'Actually, I'm not. Saul's got the money. I'm just something that can be used against him.'

'Did your parents leave you destitute?'

Shrugging, she said, 'I don't know. I suppose they left me enough to keep me out of the poorhouse, but they weren't stupid. Saul is the kingpin, the one everyone depends on; naturally he has the power.'

'What do you mean, you don't know?' He sounded sceptical.

She said defensively, 'Well, I don't.'

'Haven't been interested enough to find out, or has it been kept from you?'

'Of course it hasn't been *kept* from me! I just haven't bothered to find out, that's all. Saul——'

'You're eighteen, and you're making no attempt to train yourself to take the reins of your own affairs?' There was a thread of something perilously close to contempt in his voice, although none of it showed in his face. He tossed a lettuce over to her, saying, 'Here, wash this.'

Stephanie thrust it under the tap, shaking it mercilessly. 'I suppose you think I'm stupid.'

'I know you're not stupid. Do you expect your brother to look after you all your life?'

'Of course not!'

'Then what are you doing about it? What subjects were you going to take at university, always assuming you were planning to go there?'

She bit her lip, because although Saul wanted her to get a degree she had been tempted to follow the example of her best friend and attend a finishing school in France. 'Fine Arts,' she retorted, wrenching the lettuce apart. The crisp leaves exploded in her fingers.

'And then a stint of working at Sotheby's, I suppose,' he said curtly, 'while you find some chinless wonder to marry.'

'That's so old-fashioned.' She exaggerated her accent, clipping the words savagely to give emphasis. 'It's a new world out there now. All the chinless wonders have careers in merchant banks. And I certainly don't want to work at Sotheby's.'

'At least it's a job. How are you going to fill in your days? Lunching and going to beauty salons?'

'Don't worry, I'll manage it somehow.'

He was only repeating what Saul had been telling her for the last few years, and in a somewhat milder form, but Saul had her best interests at heart. Duke didn't even know her well enough to know what her interests were.

'You're drowning that lettuce.' He leaned over to turn off the tap. For a second she felt his closeness like the brush of something at once abrasive and potent, as stimulating as the silken texture of fur against her nerves.

Stepping back, she looked around for a bowl to dump the wet lettuce into.

'There's a colander under the sink,' he said. 'A basin with holes in it.'

'I do know what a colander is,' she said stiffly. 'I'm not completely useless.' She found it, took it as far from him as possible, and dropped the lettuce in to drain. Then she said, 'I haven't really thought about what I'll do. Saul wanted me to do a business course of some sort, but it sounds boring.'

'You've left it a bit late to decide, princess,' he said drily, wielding the knife on some tomatoes. 'By your age most people have a reasonable idea of what career they want. Wash that asparagus for me, there's a good girl.'

Anger sparked through her, an anger she kept well hidden because it seemed too strong a reaction to his observation. He had no right to assume that she was an empty-headed idiot with nothing but a good marriage on her mind; she would, she decided, walking across the stone flags to get the asparagus, show him that she was capable of doing whatever she wanted to do.

In spite of Saul's remarks she had always assumed that he would manage her finances, but it really wasn't fair to expect him to do that for the rest of her life.

When I get out of this, she decided, when I get back to real life, I'll ask Saul what he thinks would be the most helpful course for me to take, and this time I'll listen properly to him!

They ate in the kitchen at the huge scrubbed table; for the first time since Duke had hauled her back to life Stephanie enjoyed the tastes and textures of food, finishing the whole plateful. When Duke asked her whether she wanted coffee she shook her head.

'No, I don't drink it, thank you.' A yawn sneaked up from nowhere, and she said, surprised, 'I wonder why I'm so tired.'

'Today is the first day you've been up.'

Well, of course. She rose, saying as steadily as she could, because the thought of him joining her in the big bed was doing odd things to her stomach, 'So it is.' Her gaze fell on the dirty plates. 'Do you mind if I leave you with the dishes?'

'No,' he said gravely, standing.

She blinked. He was so tall, he seemed to fill her vision. Very rapidly she said, 'Goodnight.'

But he came up with her, waiting in the bedroom while she showered and pulled on the T-shirt she wore at night. He had left his dressing-gown on the back of the door; she looked at it for a moment, then left it there. Her back was very stiff as she came into the bedroom.

Not that he noticed; he was sitting in the chair, looking at a book he had brought up that morning because he thought she might be interested in it. She suspected that he'd chosen it because it was a romance. Unfortunately it was one she'd already read.

'Do you want to read for a while?' he asked, when at last she was under the duvet.

'No, not tonight.' Her tone was as distant as his, her expression as controlled.

'Then I'll go down. Don't put the light on.'

Stephanie looked up sharply. 'Did you find something out in the village?' she asked, trying to hide the note of fear in her voice.

He shook his head. 'Not a thing. Let me do the worrying, Stephanie. That's what I'm here for.'

But when he had gone she lay in the darkness, watching stars as big and clear as diamonds on rough velvet, and wondered. Something about the way he had said she wasn't to turn on the light had set alarm bells ringing. He might not be in contact with Saul, but that didn't mean he wasn't able to talk to others. Perhaps he had a scanner and had picked up some shred of information from it. Or had he overheard a remark in the village that had made him uneasy?

Because he was—well, uneasy probably wasn't the right word. He seemed electric, focused, as though all his formidable resources, physical and intelligent, were concentrated on some problem.

She was sure of it, as sure as she was that he wouldn't tell her what that problem was.

Quelling a bolt of incipient panic, she told herself that of course he'd have some sort of security system rigged. A cautious man, he called himself. He'd admitted it was highly unlikely that anyone was watching them, yet he made her stay inside and keep away from the windows just on the off-chance. Even, she thought resentfully, hauling his T-shirt down over her hips, to the extent of keeping her without clothes in case someone went through their laundry!

It was just her bad luck that he was the most compellingly attractive man she had ever met. He had that impressive aura of—authority, although it was more than that. An impregnable, leashed toughness that even his kindness couldn't hide emanated from him and set him apart.

Wincing at the ache in her thighs and calves, she stretched her legs. Stone floors were hard on muscles that hadn't been used for some days. Tomorrow she'd start exercising.

Eventually she drifted into an uncomfortable sleep, waking in the morning with a thick head and heavy eyes to the sound of something being put down on the bedside table. Normally he moved noiselessly, so he must have meant to make the little clink that woke her.

'Bad night?' he asked, straightening up. The orange juice he'd just deposited glowed brilliant in the sunny room. 'You spent quite a lot of it muttering.'

The casual comment flicked an obscure anger. He didn't need to sound so—so untouched, as though sleeping with her meant absolutely nothing to him.

But then, it didn't.

He smelt of fresh air and sunlight and the soft, ever-present fragrance of pines and grass and wild flowers.

Suddenly overcome by a hunger to escape from this silly mock-castle, from the whole dangerous charade, Stephanie said brusquely, 'Sorry,' and sat up, carefully pulling the sheet and duvet with her. 'What's it like out?'

'Glorious.' He stood observing her with the speculative scrutiny she found so unnerving. 'Getting a touch of cabin fever?'

It was maddening, the way he seemed to be able to gauge her attitudes and moods while withholding any hint of his. She drank half the glass of orange juice before answering, 'Yes.'

'Hang on to your composure for a while. I don't know how much longer this will last, but it looks now as though things are going down fast.'

'I thought you weren't in contact with Saul,' she said.

'I'm not, but I am in contact with other people,' he answered promptly, looking amused, as though he could see through her attempts to find out what was going on. 'Cheer up, princess; soon you can go back to your nice, safe cocoon with nice, well-paid minders to keep you

out of trouble, and then all of this will gradually fade
like the memory of a nightmare. You probably won't
ever forget it, but it won't ruin your life.'

The note of irony in his voice hurt damnably, but she
retorted crisply, 'I don't intend to let any greedy thugs
affect *my* life, thank you.'

His hard mouth compressed into a smile, humourless,
almost cynical. 'That's the way,' he said. 'Arrogant to
the wire. Are you coming down for breakfast, or shall
I bring it up?'

'I'll be down in ten minutes.' With narrowed eyes she
watched him leave, hating the way he called her princess,
but because she knew he expected her to demur she refused to object. A day would come, she vowed darkly
as she flung the bedclothes back, when she'd tell him
exactly how she felt about it. And about other things,
too.

After her shower she got into his dressing-gown, rolling
up the sleeves and tying the cord several times around
her thin waist before setting off down the stairs and
through the great hall.

Again they ate in the kitchen, one part of which was
chiselled out of the side of the mountain; on the other
the hill fell away abruptly to reveal a steep-sided valley
carved out by glaciers before the ice had retreated twelve
thousand years ago. Through the eastern windows the
sun streamed in a golden flood, glamorising the
workaday room with its magic.

'What did your contact tell you about the situation?'
Stephanie asked.

'It seems that your brother has everything under
control.'

'Well, of course he has,' she said absently. 'Is he any
closer to the men who actually set this kidnapping up?'

He said coolly, 'There's a possibility they may be dis-
affected members of your family who told the kidnappers to neutralise you. No, listen. Someone, as yet
unknown, is mounting an attempt to dislodge your

brother from his position as head of Jerrard's. If he
didn't know where you were, and was afraid that you
were dead, or close to it, he certainly wouldn't be giving
the bid his best attention.'

When the implications of that sank in, she put down
her knife, her appetite departing in a sickening rush.
'That's a foul thing to say! Uncle Stephen wouldn't do
that. Oh, I know he dislikes Saul, but he's family. He
wouldn't use me like that. And neither would Uncle
Edward, or Patrick.'

'It's only a possibility. Even if it's true, they almost
certainly wouldn't have intended to have you abused so
viciously,' Duke said crisply. 'They'd have wanted you
held, but they wouldn't have known what methods the
men they paid would use to do that.'

She shuddered. 'No. I don't believe it.'

'Finish your breakfast.'

She said numbly, 'I can't.'

'Yes, you can. You need to eat, princess.'

When she shook her head, he ordered inflexibly, 'Eat
it.'

Stephanie flashed him a furious look, but the cold
and controlled menace in his eyes made her blink. He
was angry, and it was not because she refused to eat her
breakfast. Uncowed, she nevertheless found herself
picking up the slice of toast and biting into it.

'The rumours may be wrong,' he said, as though the
naked exercise of power had never happened. 'Unfortunately we have to look at every possibility, not just
the ones that appeal most to you.'

She chewed that thought over with her toast. 'My
uncles might have been greedy,' she said eventually, 'and
the battle they fought for Jerrard's took some very nasty
turns, but they aren't criminals! Isn't Saul's money
enough reason for me to be kidnapped?'

'Twenty million excellent reasons.'

She picked up another piece of toast and buttered it.
'My uncles would never consider doing such a thing.

They know Saul. After what happened when my parents died,' she said at last, her voice very steady, '*everyone* knows Saul is not in the habit of being conned. And that he is very protective—ruthlessly so—where his family is concerned.'

He appeared to know what she was talking about—the merciless revenge Saul had inflicted on the men who'd thought they could use his parents in their brutal bid for power. He had hunted down every man, even the ones who had worked in the kitchen of the jungle camp that had seen his parents' last, anguished days.

'I suppose they thought that any man has his weakness.' Duke resumed his substantial breakfast. Of course a man his size would have to get through a fair amount of food just to keep that big body going.

Smiling tightly, Stephanie spread marmalade on to her toast. 'Not Saul.'

He showed his teeth in a smile that lifted the hairs on the back of her neck, but before he had time to reply there was a hearty knock on the back door, followed by a vigorous rattle of the handle.

Duke looked at her with flat, deadly eyes and said, in a chilling monotone so soft that no one more than three feet away would have been able to hear, 'Get into the pantry, and whatever happens don't make any noise.'

She leapt to her feet and raced across the stone flags. Wordlessly, unable to hear anything above the irregular thunder of her pulses, she dragged open the heavy, old-fashioned door of the pantry and dived through, closely followed by Duke with her plate and knife in his hand.

Another rap on the door made her heart leap into overdrive. As Duke called with a subtle change of inflexion, 'All right, I'm coming!' she snatched the utensils, and watched as he disappeared, closing the door softly behind him.

The lock was not the elaborate Victorian extravaganza she expected, but another smoothly turning, heavy modern one. Duke's hand on the other side sent the

deadlock home. The snick as it slid into place made
Stephanie jump; for a second the panic she had been
trying so hard to overcome surged back, tightening her
skin, sending her pulse booming in her ears. Moving with
the instinctive care of shock, she put the plate and knife
down on the bench.

Be logical, she commanded her frantic brain and body.
Of course there was no need to have a locking system
on her side of the door. This was, after all, a pantry—
butter and ham and vegetables didn't try to escape! But
trying to jeer herself out of her mindless fear didn't
produce the instant calm and clear-headedness she
craved. Perhaps the days spent in the crypt had given
her claustrophobia, because a horrible turbulence
knotted her stomach.

She sat down on a set of steps, waiting for the nausea
to recede. In a few minutes the intruder, whoever he
was—a goatherd, perhaps—would leave, and Duke
would come and let her out.

Relax, she told herself. Look around you, see what's
for dinner tonight. *Pull yourself together*!

Her dilated eyes roamed across wooden shelves lining
the wall except for where an elderly refrigerator loomed;
she sought the homely comfort of the foodstuffs, only
to realise with a jolt that the writing on the packets was
in a foreign language. German. For some strange reason
that was another blow aimed at her equilibrium.

She forced herself to continue her survey. Cupboards
with misaligned doors crouched beneath a well-scrubbed
wooden bench. High in the northern wall a narrow
window provided dim illumination. Even without the
bars that gave it the ominous look of a prison cell, it
wasn't big enough to crawl out of...

You don't have to crawl out of it, she told herself. But
the trapped desperation wouldn't go away. She had to
do something. Getting to her feet, she crept across to
the door and pressed her ear against the edge. Although
they had strange ideas about what constituted good taste,

Victorian tradesmen had built well. No matter how hard she strained, she couldn't hear anything more than a low rumble of voices through the door's solid timbers.

Defeated, she sat down again, the churning in her stomach increasing, and suddenly realised that if she hoisted the set of steps on to the bench and climbed on to them she'd be able to look out of the window. It seemed like a lifeline; she couldn't bear to crouch like this in the half-darkness, with the shelves threatening to fall down on her.

It wasn't easy, but she managed to get both the steps up and herself on to the bench without any noise. The window looked on to a kind of courtyard which had once, perhaps, led to the stables. By craning her neck she could just see the back door. She stared at it for a few moments, willing their uninvited and unwelcome guest to come through it. It remained obdurately closed.

Balked, she turned her head to glance along the other side of the wall.

It plunged down the mountainside, meeting up with a band of fir trees, dark and thick and impenetrable. Stephanie was assailed by a feeling of *déjà vu*, as though she knew this place, had climbed that slope in innumerable dreams, had smelt the scented balsam of those whispering sentinels of trees.

On the edge of her vision was a gnarled relic of the glacier moraine, a huge, twisted boulder embedded in firs. At the base of that rock, she knew, was a crevice where—where Duke had hidden her before he'd slid through the forest like a huntsman stalking his prey.

No, she thought, shutting her eyes for a moment. Rocks thrust their way through the earth's thin skin on every mountain in Switzerland. She was imagining the similarity. Her gaze drifted along the edge of the firs to a tiny white circular temple set with columns and a domed roof that nestled most incongruously against the trees.

'Oh, God,' she whispered. 'Oh, God, oh, God...'

The second time Duke had stashed her in their climb up the mountain so that he could go and reconnoitre, she had glimpsed white columns through the trees and thought she was hallucinating.

She hadn't been. The slope, the trees looked so familiar because she had actually been there. Further down, at the base of the mountain, the fir trees would press closely around an outlying stub that had been hollowed and barred to make the crypt.

The castle was only a few hundred yards up the mountainside from her prison.

A noise from the opposite direction whipped her head around. The back door had opened, and a man appeared; the sun struck his peaked cap. Dressed in nondescript clothes—grey trousers and a blue shirt with rolled-up sleeves and open neck—he didn't look like Stephanie's notion of a goatherd. He just looked ordinary, nothing frightening about him at all.

He turned and walked off through the arched tunnel that must lead to the forecourt. Behind him the door clanged shut.

Panic drove through her like a solar flare. It became imperative not to let Duke know she had seen him with the man. The inchoate suspicions she had been trying to subdue, the intuition that warned her she knew next to nothing about Duke, impelled her down. Swiftly she dragged the steps after her. She was sitting on them, chin in hand, when the deadlock began to slide back and a voice, still muffled by the heavy door, said quietly, 'Stephanie?'

She froze, licking suddenly dry lips, unable to speak. Was it Duke, or someone else? There had been no one else at the door—had two men arrived, and was Duke even now a prisoner? If he wasn't, why was he fumbling as he opened the door? Duke never made an unnecessary move; his predator's grace gave his every gesture a fluid elegance.

Without thought, she snatched the heavy wooden rolling-pin from the bench. Adrenalin pumped through her as she positioned herself to one side of the door. Tensely, she waited, panic and indecision swamped by determination. Her knuckles gleamed white on the handle of the rolling-pin; she forced herself to relax, to be ready.

'Stephanie,' the voice said again.

The door began to open. She braced herself. If there had been another man—— Then Duke walked in.

Some animal instinct warned him. Just in time to stop the rolling-pin from crashing on his head, he ducked and swung, catching her wrist in a numbing grip. The heavy wooden pin fell clattering to the floor.

For a moment they stood motionless, Stephanie's eyes imprisoned by his icy glare, her senses in top gear. His anger was a palpable, living entity in the small room, as fierce and savage as the narrowed eyes that held hers so mercilessly.

Then he smiled, and the freezing fury was gone, banished by an exercise of will that shattered her.

'Damn it,' he complained mildly, 'you could have killed me.'

'For a moment I thought—I thought it might be someone else. Why on earth didn't you say it was you?' she demanded, taking refuge in sheer rage.

'I thought you'd recognise my voice.' The mockery in the deep voice sent her blood-pressure rocketing up.

'I didn't. You scared the hell out of me,' she said robustly. 'Don't do it again!'

'No, ma'am.' He wasn't in the least meek; like his use of the word princess, the 'ma'am' emphasised his refusal to be impressed by her arrogance.

Stephanie didn't care. If he wanted to point out the distance between them she was all for it; she was far too aware of him, unbearably conscious of the pulse beating in the bronzed hollow of his throat, overwhelmed by the sheer size of him, which was both intimidating yet oddly comforting, too affected by the focused male sexuality.

The Stockholm syndrome, she thought scornfully, and asked with what she hoped sounded like crisp hauteur, 'Who was that?'

'One of the locals. He was surprised to see someone here, and wanted to make sure it wasn't squatters.'

She asked, 'Do they have squatters in Switzerland?'

'Not that I'm aware of,' he returned.

Something in the way he spoke, some faint intonation, caught her attention. She looked at him keenly, but there was nothing in his eyes, his expression, to reveal what he was thinking. 'So?' she asked on a belligerent note.

'So I'll take a look around. I don't imagine our visitor is anybody to worry about, but he could have been asked to check out the man renting the castle.'

A cold chill settled in her stomach. 'By whom?'

'We don't know that.'

Although, she thought, bristling anew, some of us have our suspicions. But, try as she might, she simply couldn't see either of her uncles, or her cousin, in a conspiracy like this.

'Remember,' he said, watching her from beneath thick lashes, 'this is all supposition. He was probably just a passing villager who doesn't indulge in gossip.'

She took a deep breath, but she had to ask. 'Why didn't you tell me this castle is just above the crypt?'

Those intense eyes settled on the steps, flicked back to her face. 'Because I knew you'd hate it,' he said casually.

She frowned, wondering whether to believe him, knowing that she mustn't appear to be overly concerned. 'But why did we have to come the long way round in the car? We could just have walked up the hill.'

He said drily, 'The trees are well back from the castle. I didn't want to carry you across the grass in full view of anyone who happened to be looking. At this time of the year there are tourists swarming like ants over every mountain in Switzerland, and tourists talk in bars and clubs.'

She nodded, but persisted, 'Surely it's dangerous? So close?'

'No. The men who kidnapped you would expect any rescuer to take you straight back to your brother. They're not likely to look for you a few hundred yards up the mountain.'

After a moment she nodded. It made sense, even though the thought of that hideous room so close by iced her blood.

'I suppose you're going to lock me in the bedroom again while you're out,' she said.

'Not this time,' he said deliberately. 'You can come with me. In the boot of the car, I'm afraid, and it will be profoundly uncomfortable, but you'll cope.'

Of course he knew that the prospect of being shut up again made her sick with a disgusting combination of helplessness and anger, but one glance at his face told her that he wasn't going to change his mind. Swallowing, she said, 'Yes, all right.'

'Go upstairs and strip everything from the bedroom and bathroom that could connect you with the place.'

'Why?'

He smiled, a meaningless movement of his mouth. 'Just in case someone decides to snoop while we're gone.'

'Oh.' So that was why they were leaving the castle. What would have been fear if Duke hadn't been there abraded her nerves.

'Leave the sheets on the bed and my stuff, but put everything you've used into this bag.'

Within a very few minutes she had emptied the room of anything that might be construed as feminine, ruthlessly stuffing her toothbrush and the hairbrush he'd provided into the plastic bag, even putting in the historical romance she'd been rereading in case they—if *they* came looking—thought it was suspiciously feminine.

When he appeared in the doorway she couldn't prevent a start. 'I wish you'd make a noise,' she said irritably. 'It's not normal for anyone to move as quietly as you do.'

'Don't go imagining kidnappers under the bed,' he advised, giving the room a swift survey. 'The man was probably exactly what he said, and I'm being over-cautious.'

Efficiently he went through the room, searching with an expertise that chilled her further. At last he smiled and said laconically, 'You've done a good job.'

'For a novice. You're a professional,' she commented without inflexion.

He looked at her. 'Yes.'

That was all, but she shivered.

'Never mind, princess,' he said quite kindly. 'It shouldn't be too long before you're safely back home.'

'I don't think I'll ever feel safe again,' she said, striving to conceal the forlorn note with a crisp no-nonsense manner.

'You will. From now on you'll be so surrounded by bodyguards you'll probably never be alone again.'

'A horrible fate,' she said gloomily.

Silently they went down to the car. Without comment Stephanie climbed into the cavity of the boot, endeavoured to get comfortable on the mattress, and closed her eyes, striving to empty her face and mind of any emotion.

'Try to sleep,' he advised tersely.

Her eyes flew open. For a moment sheer panic darkened them. And then, as he bent his head, they darkened even more. Strong hands holding her still, he pressed a kiss on her lips.

'Think about that,' he said harshly, and straightened up. The boot lid clanged down.

Stephanie lay immobile as the engine started up. Through the stunned reaches of her brain and body the glittering promise of his kiss surged like a wild, irresistible tide. Without thought, without holding anything back, her soft, untutored mouth had shaped itself to his in a response that still shimmered through her, sweet as run honey, a mindless, helpless obedience to a summons older than time.

It made her giddy with pain, because now he was well aware of the helpless attraction that clouded her judgement. His kiss had been a calculated power play, and her ardent response would have told him that his influence over her was almost limitless.

As the car eased down the steep drive she wondered what was going to happen now.

The ride seemed to go on for ages. Several times the car stopped, and once she heard the sounds of a busy village street, but the lid remained obdurately closed, and she had to stay quiescent, barely daring to breathe. Much to her astonishment, she finally managed to doze.

At last, however, the sound of the engine died, replaced by an intense silence. Once more Stephanie lay breathing shallowly. Was this merely another route stop, or were they back at the castle?

Time dragged by. Tired, uncomfortable and more than ready to call someone to account for it, she tried to dampen down the anger seething through her. She heard nothing until the lock clicked and someone opened the boot. She lay pretending to be asleep; she had already worked out that if it wasn't Duke she'd have a better chance of getting free if they thought her unconscious. However, beneath the thick fringe of her lashes she recognised his harsh-featured face, and sat up, blinking in the semi-gloom.

When she opened her mouth to ask what was going on his hand snapped out and covered it. Her eyes, already dilated, widened even further. He leaned forward and breathed into her ear, 'The place has been bugged. We have to go.'

Panic dragged her thought processes into a whirlwind. She heard her jagged intake of breath and above the hard command of his hand her gaze sought his face, frantically begging for comfort. Instead, the icy command in his eyes warned her to keep silent as he pushed her inexorably back down, deposited his bag behind the curl of her knees, and closed the lid.

Stiff and cramped, Stephanie lay fuming impotently. At first anger won out over fear, but as the car retraced its path down the side of the mountain a cold, empty pit expanded in her stomach. Exactly when it turned into active nausea she didn't know.

But Duke was with her; she clung to his image like a talisman, a charm to keep the enemy at bay. Duke wouldn't let anything happen to her.

The car was moving fast over the excellent Swiss roads. Once they went through a large town; the car slowed, stopped at several lights. She heard the sounds of revving engines, the occasional hiss of brakes, horns, wrinkled her nose at the odour of other cars' exhaust and winced at the abrupt turns of narrow streets. Once or twice the turns were so sharply taken that she was tossed around and grunted painfully as tender bits of her anatomy met the unyielding surround of the boot.

Losing track of time, she became more and more aware of an increasing discomfort that had to be contained, the very real threat of being sick, so that by the time the car stopped she was barely able to think.

The boot lid was raised. Once more they were in the gloom of a garage of some sort, but this one was smaller than the other, much cleaner and tidier, and lit only by a high window.

'OK,' Duke said soothingly, lifting her out as though she were a child. 'We're here, and as far as I can tell we haven't been followed.'

'Where's here?' she croaked.

'A safe house.'

'Safer than the last, I hope.' Goading him was dangerous, but it gave her some illusion of control.

His mouth tightened into a thin line, but when she staggered his arm came out instantly, supporting her with a rock-like strength. 'It will have to be.'

Returning feeling brought a familiar pain to her limbs. Biting her lip, she relaxed and let it wash over her as she asked, 'Did you suspect that the castle might be bugged?'

'If anyone was wanting to know about the people who lived there it seemed the logical thing to do,' he said quietly, 'so I gave them the opportunity.'

The heat from his big body enfolded her, weakening her. She pulled away, trying to unfog her brain from the memory of his kiss. She asked doggedly, 'Who are *they*?'

'We don't know their identities, but we'd be on safe ground assuming they were the ones who organised your kidnapping.'

Stephanie looked at his face, but no expression escaped the absolute control he imposed on his features. The flashfire of panic that had engulfed her for a second ebbed. 'How did they find out I was there?'

He shrugged. 'I don't know. At least we were ready for them. We'll have to be even more careful here.'

'How do you know no one followed us? Surely that's what they'd have done? It's what I'd have done.'

He looked down into her face. She read a tough, unwavering confidence in his honed features. 'Two cars took it in turns,' he said casually. 'I gave them the slip in Lucerne; by the time they backtrack—if they manage to do it—the trail will be stone-cold.' He urged her towards a door.

Stephanie asked sharply, 'Does Saul know we're here?'

'Yes.' His voice was cool and controlled, giving nothing away.

They were in a modern house, small and white and clean, a chalet with geraniums and begonias brilliant in boxes outside windows shielded by net curtains. On the ground floor the rooms ran into one another, so that they stepped from the garage into a colourful, pretty kitchen and dining-room, and thence to a sitting-room with a panelled front door opening directly into it and a spiral staircase in one corner. There was very little furniture in the place, but its very sparseness after the fake antiquities in the castle gave it a charm Stephanie warmed to. Like the castle it was on the side of a mountain, and outside on the alp the grass was starred with flowers, their bright forms emphasised by the setting sun.

Duke had been watching her, noting her quick survey. Once in the neat sitting-room, he said, 'Never mind, princess, it's almost over. You'll be back home soon.'

'You've been saying that right from the start,' she said half angrily, staring at the blank face of the television screen as though she could see her future in it. 'I'm sick of platitudes. Why won't you tell me anything?'

'Because,' he said deliberately, 'if by some remote chance they recapture you, I don't want you to know anything. That way, you can't be forced to spill any beans.'

Almost, she thought hollowly, she'd prefer evasions, even lies, to this brutal bluntness.

'I see,' she said.

'But that's not going to happen,' he said, and for a moment she thought there was sympathy and understanding in his deep voice. 'It's just that I'm a cautious man.'

She was getting heartily sick of that phrase. 'I need a shower,' she said.

'All right.'

'I wasn't asking permission,' she flashed.

Dark brows shot up. Those piercing, crystalline eyes made a leisurely survey of her flushed face. 'No, I can see that,' he observed.

Immediately ashamed, she said reluctantly, 'I'm sorry. I'm a bit—jittery.'

'You're allowed to be.'

The tone of his voice relegated her to the nursery. She could almost see the words 'spoilt, arrogant child' forming in his brain, and felt like bursting into tears and indulging in a proper tantrum, something she had never done even as a child.

CHAPTER FIVE

As THEY walked up the stairs Stephanie found herself wondering about the difference she discerned in Duke. Outwardly there was none. He appeared the same—invulnerable, guarded, the uncompromising angles and planes of his face proclaiming an unreachable, adamantine man totally in command of himself and the situation.

Yet senses more discriminating and perceptive than sight assured her that he had changed. He was waiting, she thought, for something he knew was going to happen, alert, poised to respond instantaneously and ruthlessly.

The stairs finished in an open landing with two bedrooms opening off it; the one above the sitting-room was a big, dormitory-style affair, separated by a bathroom from another with a double bed.

'In here,' Duke said, opening the door into the smaller room.

She asked, 'What do we do now?'

'Nothing.' His smile was narrow, mirthless. 'Just what we've always done, princess. We leave the work to others.'

'You'd rather be one of those others, wouldn't you?' He wouldn't tell her, but she was trying to keep her mind off her queasiness. Possibly the exhaust that had penetrated the boot in whatever city they'd passed through had affected her; certainly something had made her stomach a battleground.

His brows climbed. 'Don't you think I make a good nursemaid?'

The ironic undertone told her that he hated this inactivity.

She said honestly, 'You make a brilliant rescuer and knight-errant. I may never be able to thank you enough.'

One corner of the hard mouth lifted. 'Don't even try,' he advised. 'Think of yourself as part of my career path.'

Stephanie laughed, as he'd meant her to. 'All right, but just the same—you've been very kind, and I am truly grateful. I won't ever forget what you've done for me, and neither will my brother.'

Even as the words left her lips she knew it was the wrong thing to say. Not that his expression changed, but she felt the sudden chill, the instant, unyielding withdrawal.

'Even better for my career path,' he said, that faint hint of another accent very much to the fore in each drawled word.

His New Zealand connections must be close to have given that flavour to his pronunciation. Embarrassment at her *faux pas* sent heat crawling across her cheekbones. She said clumsily, 'I didn't mean it like that, and you know it.'

'Then what did you mean?' he asked, refusing to allow her any face-saving evasion.

She wished she'd shut up. Her blue eyes shifted sideways, then came back to his face. 'All right,' she said crossly, 'I suppose I did. If it's hurt your pride I'm sorry. But I *am* very grateful, and I always will be.'

'Always,' he said with an odd, humourless, enigmatic smile, 'is a very long time, princess. Don't make promises like that.' And the cold, corroding anger she had sensed disappeared. Now totally businesslike, he said crisply, 'All right, you must be exhausted. Have your shower, and then get into bed. Just remember there's only supposed to be me in the house.'

A fundamental element in their relationship had altered. Her unsubtle promise of material rewards hadn't caused the change, although, she thought miserably, it hadn't helped. Except that she hadn't meant the reward to be financial; she barely knew what she had meant, and at the moment she shied away from searching her soul for the answer.

Perhaps his kiss had done the mischief. No; she would always remember the heart-stopping intimacy of it, but she was sure it had meant nothing to him. He had kissed with skill and bone-melting expertise, so there had been plenty of other women in his life. Her mouth tilted wryly, defensively as she told herself that one kiss pressed on an eighteen-year-old wasn't going to tilt his equilibrium.

But the slightly mocking camaraderie had been replaced by a steely inflexibility. Possibly his professional pride was hurt. After all, he had promised to keep her safe, and although he'd kept his promise they'd been driven from the castle.

Unable to respond to the cheerful surroundings, so different from the castle's mock-Gothic splendour, she looked around the bedroom with a heavy heart. This was like a doll's-house, fresh and small and newly painted, although most dolls'-houses had far more elaborate furnishings than this. Here there was only a bed and a shiny cream wardrobe.

The grabbing bitterness in her stomach urged her towards the tiny bathroom. If she was going to be sick she wanted some privacy for it. 'I'll have that shower,' she gabbled.

'A good idea. I'll be back in a few minutes with some food.'

Once she was in the shower the nausea decreased so swiftly that by the time she had dried herself and her hair she was feeling much better. Nevertheless, she obeyed Duke's command and got into the bed, although when he appeared with a tray she said, 'I'm not hungry, Duke.'

'Tension,' he said calmly. 'Eat up, there's a good kid.'

'I'm not a kid!'

His dark brows drew together. 'Then act like a mature adult,' he said coolly, 'and refuel. You went without lunch; you must be hungry.'

Perhaps he was right. It could be lack of food that was making her stomach grumble testily. Sullenly, knowing she was behaving badly yet unable to stop herself, she lifted the knife and fork and ate while Duke stood watching. She felt like a child told that it couldn't leave the table until its plate was clean.

It didn't help matters that he was right; she did feel much better, at least physically, for the food.

'What's your problem?' he asked, startling her.

Seized by a temptation to tell him exactly what her problem was—in order, she realised, that he could convince her she was wrong—she drained the last of the too sweet orange juice and muttered, 'I'm frightened, I suppose. I want this to be over, life to be the way it was before.'

Wide shoulders moved in a slight shrug beneath the fine cotton of his shirt. 'Life will never be the same again,' he said dispassionately. 'You're setting yourself up for a fall if you think it will be. You can never go back. That doesn't mean you can't be happy, because of course you can, but it won't be the same happiness.'

Stephanie darted him a resentful look. The forceful features were completely without sympathy. Not for him any easy, lying platitudes.

'I know,' she said, capitulating. She added with a painful smile, 'I suppose I just want my mummy.'

His answering smile was wryly sympathetic. 'I know the feeling. It will soon pass, and in the meantime you need rest. Try to get some.'

She waited until he had left the room before lying back, but almost immediately knew that whatever was wrong with her stomach was not lack of food.

Ten minutes later she walked quietly out of the bathroom, relieved that he hadn't come up to check on her. Now that her stomach was empty she felt amazingly better, but tired.

Almost immediately exhaustion and emotion overtook her, and she dropped off to sleep, waking much later with a dry mouth and an incipient headache. An automatic glance at her naked wrist made her decide angrily that she was going to demand a watch. It wasn't the first time she'd wanted to know the time, and apart from finding it infuriating she hated being without any of the familiar things that reinforced her identity. However, the room was dark with the shadows of evening, so she had slept for quite a long time. Turning her head, she saw that the other side of the bed was empty, so it couldn't be too late.

At least, she thought after an experimental check on her well-being, the gripe in her stomach had gone. A headache nagged dully behind her brows, making her brain sluggish and thick, and in her mouth there lingered a faint, unpleasant taste, but she felt a lot fitter than she had when she'd gone to sleep.

Yawning, she slid out of the bed, went into the bathroom, and got a glass of water. It ran cool and refreshing down her throat, and she felt much better, good enough to go downstairs. Duke's dressing-gown hung on the back of the door; she shrugged into it, tied it around her waist, rolled up the sleeves and set off.

The house was so still, she almost expected to find the door on to the narrow upper landing locked, but it opened without impediment, swinging back silently. Nevertheless she hesitated, the hairs on the back of her neck lifting.

You're being utterly stupid, she told herself. Go on, go down, right now.

But she lifted her feet slowly, carefully as she walked out on to the landing.

And then she stopped, because voices floated up the spiral stairs. Muted voices, so that she couldn't hear the words, but voices nevertheless. And something in the timbre told her that Duke wasn't simply watching television or listening to the radio, although there was the sound of electronic conversation in the background, conversation in another language.

Over the sound of the Swiss German, someone—not Duke—was talking in English.

Panic thickened her throat, caught her by the nerves and strangled her, so that she stood frozen and witless until some atavistic survival instinct smashed the shackles of horror. If Duke was in danger she was damned well going to do something about it, not die of fright.

Holding her breath, she crept towards the top of the staircase, carefully avoiding the edge so that she couldn't be seen. After strained moments of hearing no distinguishable words, she lowered herself to the floor. Surprisingly, the position seemed to sharpen her hearing.

'Right,' Duke said, his voice imperturbable, and she relaxed, only to tense again when he went on, 'So tell me what's so important that you had to come here. And make it quick. I gave her a knock-out pill to keep her under, but I'm a cautious man and I don't trust them.'

'I came here to tell you that someone followed you.'

'I know,' Duke said impatiently. 'You did.'

'And one of Jerrard's men.'

'Rubbish. I'd have seen him.'

'Perhaps you're not such a good getaway man as you thought.' Satisfaction tinged the other man's tone. 'Because he's here.'

Stephanie knew that voice. It belonged to the younger of the two men who had kidnapped her, the one who had wanted to rape her and found her helpless, shackled resistance funny. For one hideous moment the blood drained from her head. She shook it impatiently. She felt so slow, so stupid...

Duke's voice echoed hollowly in her ears. 'Who is he?'

'Hell, how should *I* know? Calls himself Nicholson. He's Jerrard's man, that I do know. He was one of the ones closing in on the castle. Sounder recognised him— he ran across him couple of years ago.'

Duke cursed.

'Yeah, well, he's here, so you're going to have to kill the girl and get up to the top road as soon as you can.

And don't waste any time about it. Jerrard's lot are going to be here in spades before the night's over.'

Shaking, her heart thundering loudly in her ears, Stephanie closed her eyes. More than anything she wanted to believe that this was a dream, that those terrifying words were simply grim fantasies caused by an overheated imagination, the aftermath of her imprisonment in the locked crypt. She couldn't bear the wait until Duke spoke. Each moment seemed to stretch out, to dance crazily on the edge of eternity, until the sound of his voice, cool and indifferent, crashed against her eardrums.

'Bloody hell,' he said dispassionately.

'I wouldn't mind giving you a hand. The bitch fought like hell when we snatched her,' the other man said nonchalantly. 'She managed to rip Sounder's Balaclava off, and he's not too keen to have her testify in court. Or to have her brother know who he is. He's got a reputation for revenge, has Jerrard.' So matter-of-fact was his tone that Stephanie's doubts oozed away. He laughed. 'He wrapped those dagoes that killed his parents up in tinsel and handed them to the law. Most of them got a firing squad. He'll do the same to us if she's still around to identify anyone. You'll be the first they find. Not too many men of your build around. Anyway, we can do without the publicity.'

He paused, then asked with sly malice, 'Squeamish, Duke.'

'A bit,' Duke admitted without emotion. 'I don't like killing women. However, it will be easy enough to smother her. And what do I do with her body?'

'There's a pit in the garage. Leave the car over it. Looking for her should keep them busy for a couple of days,' he said cheerfully.

Even through her horror, Stephanie noticed the alteration in the newcomer's voice. Now he sounded matey, almost friendly, as though Duke's cold-blooded lack of concern had calmed some suspicion.

'What's she like in the sack? Bit skinny for my liking, but she looked as though she could be quite tasty. I wouldn't have minded a go at her myself—I've never had a rich bitch—but we saw a couple of bloody hikers in the woods when we were carrying her to that weird dungeon. They didn't see us, but he's a bit of an old woman, is Sounder, and he threatened to lock me in with her when I suggested a quick tumble.'

Duke said nothing, and the second man continued in a slightly dampened manner, 'Not that I care. When this is all over there's going to be money like you've never thought of before. We'll be as rich as Jerrard ourselves, and the girls'll be lining up to get into our beds.'

Duke laughed. 'That's worth a bit of grief,' he said easily. 'Right, you'd better get out of here.'

The other man said something so crude that Stephanie quite literally didn't believe her ears, then laughed. 'All right, I'm going.'

Stephanie had thought she was so shocked that nothing could have added to her terror. She discovered now that she was wrong. Something inhuman in Duke's tone when he'd spoken of killing her, at once casual and merciless, screwed her fear up a further, unbearable notch.

Soft sounds of movement coming towards her brought her heart into her mouth. Oh, God, were they coming up the stairs? The sound of a door opening made her sag with relief. No, they were going out the front—why didn't they go through the garage so she could make a break for it through the front door?

Not daring to breathe, she inched forward, peered over the edge. Duke stood in the doorway.

Go *on*, she thought, willing him to move out. Please, God, let him go out, so I can——

He said something and stepped back in, closing the door. Stephanie shrank back as he turned, but he didn't look up. Instead, he went across to the television and turned the sound up. He sat down in a chair, his back to the staircase.

She eased away from the edge and crawled back into the bedroom, her mind clamped into impotent anguish by the sudden, appalling truth. It was too much to have her latent suspicions flushed so brazenly into the open. She had to get out of here, and it looked as though the only way she could do it was through the window.

Holding her breath, she made her way across the room, testing the casement with cautious fingers. It was now dark, and she could see nothing but the faint glow of light from the downstairs windows on the grass. Desperately she heaved on the window-frame, but she couldn't force it past a certain distance, and there was no way she could climb through the narrow gap. She was a prisoner, had always been a prisoner.

A hideous thought struck her. Had it been *Duke* who set up the whole situation? Had he arranged the brutal kidnapping, the will-sapping time spent in the claustrophobic darkness, to establish a docile hostage he didn't need to watch nearly so closely?

Somehow she had to get out of this neat little prison. What was she going to *do*?

In books hostages seemed to find ways out of their predicaments with astonishing inventiveness, but her mind was totally blank. Not only that, she had fallen so rapidly into some sort of emotional dependency on Duke that in spite of the evidence of her ears she was still trying to find some logical reason for his words.

She had told him things about herself that she'd never divulged before, had slept in his arms with the trust and faith of a baby. Wincing, she thought she'd been utterly pathetic, her need for security conspiring against the cooler dictates of her brain.

Because her suspicions had been roused early. Stupidly, she'd let him disarm them. And now he was going to kill her. If she got out of this she was never ever going to let her hormones guide her behaviour again. At least she had one thing on her side; her bout of nausea had stopped the knock-out pill before it was able to plunge her into deep unconsciousness.

It must have been in the orange juice, she thought, tasting again the sweet sickliness.

Her heart pumped like bullets in her chest, forcing adrenalin through her bloodstream as she stepped hastily back. She stood motionless, drinking in the sweet night air, cudgelling her brain for help.

Prince of ice had been right, but prince of lies was even more appropriate. It explained things that had kept nagging at the back of her mind: his refusal to take her home to Saul, the fact that she had no clothes and had to wear his T-shirts or go naked, the insistence on secrecy...

And the keys. Of course he'd been able to get the keys to open the crypt, and the box, and the handcuffs.

Her hand stole up to her throat, covering the rattling pulse there as though she could calm it down by touch.

Oh, God, she had been such a fool! Oh, God, oh, God, oh, God...

Her thoughts jangled endlessly around inside her skull while panic caught her in its sticky clutches.

Think, she told herself. For God's sake, think! Forget that he's been kind, ignore the fact that he's rescued you from hell, looked after you—Duke is the enemy.

And in spite of his pragmatic distaste for it, he was going to kill her. Stupefied by the mixture of panic and shame that surfaced so quickly in her mind, she pressed her lips together to hold back a scream and began to search the room silently for something to defend herself with.

So he turns you on, she told herself, using scorn and contempt to defeat the terror. That's all right; you're not the first woman to be excited by a murderer. At least you've got a chance...

Hastily she scanned the wardrobe, glancing over her shoulder from time to time in case he was coming up the stairs with those noiseless steps.

Nothing in the wardrobe. Moving swiftly, noiselessly, she crouched to look under the bed.

People could do the most atrocious things for money, or for power, or for their beliefs.

Girls at school had pretended to be her friends because she was rich, some of them weaving so seamless a fabric of deceit that she had been entirely taken in; women had pretended to love her brother, eyeing his assets with greedy glances as they'd cooed at her, spoken lying words of adoration to him.

Nothing under the bed. Hurriedly, she tiptoed into the bathroom. By now her eyes were accustomed enough to the dark to be able to see quite well, but even so the only thing that in any way approximated to a weapon was her toothbrush, and that was a pitiful weapon against Duke.

She stood with her hand against her mouth, keeping back a primitive cry of outrage and pain.

Nothing else, not even a hair brush, or a heavy book.

Duke must have set her up in the pantry to see whether she would actually defend herself. Once he knew she would, he'd made sure the cupboard was bare. Well, the toothbrush was better than nothing. If she managed to thrust it into his eye...

The prospect made her feel sick, but she clung to the image, trying to psych herself into the right frame of mind.

She crept back to the staircase, but he was still watching television. Once more in the room, she searched yet again for something to hit him with, but there was nothing she could use. The wardrobe had no drawers she could pull out. Her fingers clenched on the toothbrush.

Fear kicked hard in the pit of her stomach. Each moment that went by brought her closer to her death, and she couldn't do anything about it.

She was crouching by the window trying to make out the mechanism that kept it closed when she saw the lights below go out. Whatever reprieve she'd had was over. Well, she thought defiantly as she stood up and raced across to the bathroom, she was damned if she was going to make it easy for him. The only hope she had was that he'd admitted to being squeamish. She was awake, not lost in drugged sleep; it wasn't going to be as easy as a pillow over her face while she slept.

Just possibly, he wouldn't be able to do it.

While she had been wrestling with the window an idea had popped into her brain, an idea she'd examined with avid urgency. If she could lure Duke into making love… Both men and women were at their most vulnerable then. There were ways to disable a man for long enough to give her a fighting chance.

He appeared in the doorway, a darker thickening of the darkness, coalescing out of the night like some demon lover. She knew then. The danger she was in was real and clear; she could sense his tension across the room, the subtle change of his body chemistry. Her hair stood up all over her skin, pulled tight by thousands of minuscule muscles left over from primeval times, and the quick fix of fear-induced hormone cleared her brain miraculously. Until then she had been operating on mixed signals, unable to believe that he really meant her harm; now she knew, and her mind and body joined forces.

'What's the matter?' he asked harshly, coming into the room.

The drug. He'd expected her to be sleepy and dazed. 'Something woke me,' she said, yawning, making her voice slow and stupid. 'I had a drink of water. I was so thirsty.'

She couldn't see him, but she could feel him relax.

'Sorry, I should have turned the television down,' he said smoothly, coming across to her. 'Hop back into bed.'

For a moment she wavered, then said drowsily, 'My legs won't carry me.'

He hesitated before catching her up in his strong arms. How could he be so evil when he held her so sweetly, so tenderly?

'Why have you got your toothbrush clutched in your hand?' he asked, sounding amused. Or trying to sound amused, she thought shrewdly.

'My mouth tasted nasty,' she said, as though that explained it. Afraid that he might realise why she had it, she murmured his name in as sultry a voice as she could manage. As she felt his breath lift his chest she turned with a fluidity of motion she had never experienced before and, driven by instincts that had lain waiting for this moment, kissed the hollow in his throat where his pulse beat heavily.

'Stephanie?'

For the first time ever she had succeeded in surprising him. She had to hold that element of surprise. 'Dear Duke. You're so good to me...'

With something like hope she felt the involuntary reaction that scorched through him, a response that had evaded the reins of his will. *Yes*, she thought, dazed by her success. This was the way to do it. First the seduction, and then the swift, crippling knee to the groin...

She followed that swift, tentative kiss with others across the neck of his shirt, until he dropped her into the bed, saying grimly, 'Stop this, Stephanie.'

The toothbrush went under the pillow. Making herself sound bewildered, she pulled him down. 'Why, what's the matter?'

Although he hadn't been expecting it and she might have caught him off-balance, she suspected that he came down on to the bed because he wanted to, and for a moment her resolve faltered.

She set her jaw. She was going to use woman's oldest weapon, the persuasive lure of her sexuality, to get out of this deadly trap, and then, she thought as she ran her hand up his arm and over the taut muscle of one broad shoulder, she was never going to trust another man again.

Making that initial caress was shamefully easy because, although her brain understood that she was in dire danger from this man, his dynamic masculinity clouded her resolution. Common sense whispered despairingly, but the last flickering warning of her conscious mind was close to being wiped out by the blatant electioneering of her own body.

Although she almost yielded to the heated tide of passion that rolled over her, and her breath shuddered in her lungs as she pressed her body against the powerful length of his, she knew what she was doing, and why. Like all whores, she thought wearily, she had to make sure he got his money's worth while she kept possession of her wits. It was like being split between her brain and her body.

Detachment didn't come without effort. One Stephanie kept guard while the other drowned in sensation, no longer resisting the feral need that clawed and pierced. Mute anger drove her to bite him, setting sharp white teeth to the ridge of his collarbone, then licking delicately along the mark. He tasted of salt, and musk, and the evocative flavour of male, primitive and wild.

'Stop that,' he said, but a deep, slow sensuality in his voice told her that she had won.

'Make me,' she retorted, and lowered her head to find the hard little point of his nipple. His chest lifted and for the first time in her life she heard the excited thunder of a man's heart.

He groaned something, the noise echoing in her ear, and when she moved sinuously against him he finally surrendered, an impatient hand beneath her chin lifting her face so that he could kiss her. His mouth was rapacious, hungry, as he made himself master of hers, returning fire with fire.

Body and mind duelled in a fierce, silent battle; her mind won, but barely, and then only because it occurred to her that he might use this moment to kill her.

So her shiver as his mouth took hers again in a kiss beyond desire was only partly caused by passion. Somehow, she thought confusedly, the keen edge of danger intensified everything, forced her responses into unnatural and all-consuming intensity.

And perhaps, although she didn't understand how, a naïve corner of her heart still trusted that he wasn't the callous professional criminal he had seemed to be, but the man who had cared for her and comforted her and held her warm in his arms to keep the nightmares at bay.

When he kissed her throat and ran a shaking hand down her shoulder and over her breasts, it was not entirely fear and outrage that made her shiver.

'I was afraid of this,' he said in a gritted voice that told her how savagely he was struggling for control. 'Stephanie, you're too sleepy to know what you're doing.'

'I've wanted this since that first night.' Her slurred tones held nothing but complete conviction.

'I know,' he said, his voice rough and intense, 'but we can't, not now.'

'Why?'

She held her breath, but instead of answering her fears he said, 'Because you don't really know what you're doing. Go back to sleep, my little love, and if you still feel the same way tomorrow morning we'll do something about it.'

His fingers tightened deliciously on her breast, as though he was reluctant to leave her. She arched against him, gave an involuntary wiggle of her hips, and felt the sudden tension in his big body, the quick, indrawn breath.

'No,' she said huskily. 'Now, Duke, now,' and she wriggled against him again, feeling the hard ridge that told her how aroused he was.

His mouth crushed hers, forcing it open, exploring the sweet depths as he responded to her provocation with a strong thrust of his narrow hips.

Sensation shot through her, violent and uncontrollable, like a flashfire. At that moment she wanted nothing more than to take him so deep inside her that he would no more think of killing her than he would of killing himself.

Lifting his head, he kissed the length of her throat, his mouth a heated brand against the smoothness of her skin. Exulting, Stephanie traced down the tense muscles of his back, pulling him into her, cradling him in the bowl of her hips—and felt the keys in his hip pocket. And although the fire and urgency in her blood didn't fade, the red tide receded from her brain and she knew that this was her chance. She slid her hand into his pocket, kissed the side of his throat and said, 'These are going to be uncomfortable in a minute,' and took the keys out.

His head came up, but when she dropped them on to the floor he kissed her again, this time on the sensitive hollow beneath her ear. Swallowing, because she could feel her control slipping away from her down silken paths of physical pleasure, she sent her hand past his lean hip, and onwards.

Remembering what a friend had told her about teasing a man, she stilled her fingers before deliberately stroking across the straining flesh. She had read books; she had listened to more experienced girls discuss the male psyche; she just hoped that everyone was right when they said that men were at the mercy of their hormones.

His body clenched and his arms clamped her against him, but at the moment of her triumph he reimposed his will. She felt the methodical relaxation of his muscles, the implacable energy with which he fought his battle with the desire that had seemed to have him so completely in thrall. He rolled over on to his back and said gutturally, 'No.'

Fear propelled her across him in an abandoned sprawl, spread her out on top of him; fear drove her kiss. She sank into complete carnal enjoyment of the tastes and flavours of his mouth, relishing the primitive power of his hunger beating through him to her, carrying her off with its consuming intensity.

And then, when it was almost too late, she took her opportunity. It took a supreme effort of will, but it was with all her strength that her knee came up, catching him in the one vulnerable part of his anatomy, and as he jerked and grunted with the ferocious pain she remembered something she had seen on television once and hit him across the throat with the edge of her hand. He slumped, and she flew off the bed, scooping the knot of keys from the floor.

He lay so still that she had to spend a precious second feeling for his breath; in spite of everything, her heart jumped at the rise and fall of his chest. Driven now by an imperative need to survive, she ran from the room and down the stairs, praying that the first key would open the door.

To her complete astonishment it did, which was lucky because she could hear Duke at the head of the stair, his voice thick and distorted as he called her name. God, how difficult was it to knock him out cold? He had to be made of iron. Panic and a queer sort of shame shook her hands as she pushed the door open and slipped through. She pulled hard on it, but her heart thudded high in her throat as she realised it hadn't locked.

He was far too close, moving with his usual lethal speed, showing no sign of the body-blow she had given him as he burst through the doorway. Even as she ran Stephanie knew she'd muffed her chance of escape, but she forced her legs to cover the ground, bare feet stinging on the road, her breath clattering noisily in her chest.

Suddenly, out of the darkness a flat, vicious crack seared her eardrums and at the same instant something whined past. Pain knocked her sideways, flung her off the road and into the black shelter of the firs. More pain rocketed through her shoulder and the side of her head where she'd been catapulted into an overhanging branch,

but her cry was muffled by the heavy weight of Duke's
body and the hard imperative of his hand across her
mouth. She thought he had shot her, but in those moments crushed beneath him she realised that he had saved
her from whoever was shooting.

A soft, ghostly whisper from down the hill froze her
into terrified stupor. 'Stephanie!'

Instinctively she flinched, but Duke forced her face
further into the dry leaf litter on the ground. She felt
the movements of his chest as he fought to control his
breathing. Desperately she tried to pull his hand from
her mouth, but when his other hand came around and
gripped her throat in a menacing signal she stopped
struggling.

For long moments they lay there. Stephanie could
smell sweat mingled with the scent of her own fear, feel
Duke's alertness, as keen as that of a hunted animal.

And then Duke got to his feet and pushed her
sprawling against the trunk of a fir. Stars swung and
catapulted around her head. Her quickly extinguished
yelp cut through the cool night air. Cowering, a hand
pressed against her cheek, she opened her eyes enough
to see two men facing each other, one crouched in the
classical unarmed combat position, the other, Duke by
his size, motionless a few feet away.

What happened next was imprinted in her mind along
with the scent of the fir trees on the crisp mountain air.
A blur of motion knocked the first man to the ground.
He didn't have a hope, she thought confusedly. One
moment Duke had been still as a great predator, lean
and cat-like in the darkness, and the next he was speed
and savagery and brutal efficiency.

Terrified, she began to crawl down the slope. Another
shot sang past her; this time there was no mistake. Duke
was trying to shoot her. She huddled along the ground,
the coppery taste of blood and fear in her mouth, her
face pressed once more into the fragrant leaf litter.

The man on the ground lay without moving. Fighting nausea, Stephanie tried to ascertain whether Duke had murdered him in front of her. The whine of another bullet too close by made her jump again. She closed her eyes in terror. After long moments she opened them again. Duke was standing with his back to her, his head moving slowly as he looked between the trees. And then he was gone, melting into the darkness as silently as a shadow, leaving her as noiselessly as a wounded beast seeking sanctuary. Leaving her to die?

A slight sound dragged her head around. Someone was coming through the fir trees, moving quietly but with speed. Panic kicked deep inside her; she tried not to breathe, tried to still the reverberating tattoo of her heartbeat.

And then the man coming through the wood said her name, and it was Saul. She breathed his name. Instantly Saul raced towards her, catching her as she stumbled to her feet, holding her tight in the warm sanctuary of his arms. But almost immediately he demanded, speaking close to her ear, 'Where is he? The man who was with you?'

'I don't know.' He pulled her behind the inadequate shelter of a fir trunk, shielding her with his body as she whispered, 'He's got a gun.'

'Was he shooting at you?'

She swallowed. 'Yes.'

Saul swore savagely beneath his breath, then asked, 'Are you all right?'

'Yes, none of the bullets hit me, but there's a man on the ground.' Who chose that moment to moan, thereby relieving her immensely. She had been grappling with the knowledge that she had let Duke kill him without lifting a hand to help; now she knew he was alive she relaxed a little, only to tense again when two other men appeared, both with blackened faces, both carrying what to her horrified eyes seemed to be rifles.

'It's Halliday,' one of the new arrivals said, dropping on to his knees beside the man on the ground. 'He doesn't seem to have been too damaged. No broken bones.'

'All right, pick him up. We'd better get out of here before someone comes up from the village to see what's going on. I'd rather not try to explain to the Swiss police what this is all about.' Saul kissed her cheek. 'Come on, darling, not much longer.'

She hesitated. Duke might still be within a few feet of them, waiting for an opportunity to disarm the two able-bodied men and snatch both Saul and her.

Only he wasn't. Something impalpable, something sharp and significant, had gone from the atmosphere.

'Come on,' Saul said again. 'We'll head for the helicopter. Quietly.'

He was wonderfully kind to her, and he stayed kind on the trip across the darkened continent to England; he was kind to her when he made her talk the whole thing through in the days that followed. Candace was kind, everyone was kind; even the police and the men who seemed to have no identity but asked the most penetrating questions were kind in an absent way.

'I feel such a fool,' she said miserably to Candace several days afterwards, when the flow of people who wanted to ask her questions seemed to have dried up. 'Just because he said he knew Saul I trusted him. He said I had the same eyes, and that I looked like the Jerrards.'

Candace took her hand and squeezed it hard. 'You had a very lucky escape,' she said with a shiver. 'He sounds terrifyingly clever.'

'I should have known. I did wonder. When he said that the uncles might be behind it, I refused to believe that.'

'I should jolly well think so! Your uncles would have had a fit if they'd known what happened to you. It was clever of him to use them, though. He must have known a lot about us.'

'Not necessarily,' Stephanie said bitterly. 'I told him about the battle for Jerrard's. He used it against me when it was convenient.' She turned to her brother. 'Saul, I have to know—was Andrew Hastings deliberately rammed in his car so his parents would hurry back to England?'

Saul looked grim. 'It looks like it. The maid was definitely in someone's pay; she doesn't know whose. All she could tell us what that a nice gentleman—a tall gentleman—gave her a couple of hundred pounds to tell him what you were doing, and to suggest you eat at the restaurant that night. He fed her a nice line about a secret lover arranging a surprise. She's not very bright.'

Stephanie put her hands over her eyes. 'I'll never forgive myself,' she said in a muffled voice.

'Darling, you can't take the sins of others on your shoulders.' Candace gave her a hug. 'It's not your fault.'

'If it's anyone's fault,' Saul said, 'it's mine for not looking after you better.'

'It's not yours either,' Candace said robustly. 'Both of you suffer from that well-known Jerrard syndrome, an over-developed sense of responsibility. Stop indulging it right now.'

Stephanie smiled. 'I still feel responsible for Halliday,' she said. 'How is he?'

Her brother got to his feet. 'He's recovering. He didn't take much damage—a chop to the neck that could have killed him. Either it was judged to a nicety, or misjudged.'

The same chop she had used to try and disable Duke. No, she wouldn't think of Duke…

Everyone continued being wonderfully kind to her in the weeks and months that followed, when no one found any trace of the kidnappers, or ever discovered what had happened to the man who called himself Duke.

The prince of lies…

Everyone told her she would get over it, and, of course, she did. It took her a while, but eventually she managed to overcome her residual fear, the pain that had ripped her life into shreds, and the shame that niggled away beneath her other emotions.

However, she never forgot. Occasionally she woke in the night to find herself crying, weeping vainly for something she had never had, for a man who had never existed, for a love that was merely a cruel illusion.

CHAPTER SIX

'SAUL?' Stephanie's voice was amused and astonished.

Her brother lifted his head. Blazing eyes the rare, clear colour of a sapphire took in the letter in her hand. 'What is it?'

'It's from a man who wants to name a rose after me. He says it's exactly the same colour as my hair. How does——' she consulted the expertly typed letter again '—Adam Cowdray know what colour my hair is?'

Saul's eyes sharpened. 'Adam Cowdray?' he said softly, and flicked a glance at his heavily pregnant wife, who was slowly consuming a piece of toast with an absent, inward expression. 'Dear heart, have you heard of a rose-breeder called Adam Cowdray?' he asked.

Candace, in the seven years since she had married Saul, had transformed the gardens of the various Jerrard residences around the world into recognised showpieces. The glorious tropical vista that spread around them now was a tribute to her skill. The English accent she had picked up from her husband and sister softened and deepened by the underlying New Zealand drawl, she answered, 'Of course I've heard of him. Met him, too. The firm's a New Zealand institution, but it's known worldwide. His father produced some wonderful flowers. Maniopoto was one of his, and First Dawn, and rumours have it that the son has inherited his eye and his skill at breeding. Cowdray roses usually do better in milder climates, although his Hinemoa was a real hit at Chelsea a couple of years ago.' Mischief curled her mouth. 'So was the man. Even my unsusceptible heart went pitter-pat, while Lavinia Potts-Neville almost dropped at his feet. One of those magnificent males who

116

don't look as though they've just stepped out of *Gentlemen's Quarterly*!'

Saul's brows shot up. 'Did you like him?'

'Oh, yes. He was very pleasant, and didn't freeze me off as abruptly as he did all the others. Although that was probably because he's a New Zealander too. We Kiwis stick together.'

'It could also be that you're very beautiful,' Saul said, the hint of steel in his tone sending Stephanie's brows upwards in turn. It still surprised her that he could show jealousy, even though he knew that his wife was as besotted with him as he was with her.

'Only in your eyes,' Candace said amiably, but something in her tone, in her eyes made Stephanie feel an intruder.

She should, she thought as she put the letter down and picked up a mango, be accustomed to it by now. Although she had her own apartment in London, she spent a lot of time with her brother and his wife and family in the house in the Home Counties that had been the Jerrards' base for centuries. And when Candace had decided that she would like this baby to be born in Fala'isi, the idyllic island in the South Pacific where they holidayed at least once a year, Stephanie had offered to come too, so that as the last months passed Candace would have company. Although Saul stayed close to his wife at all times, in his position some travel was essential.

'*Not* over the breakfast-table,' she said crisply now. 'Behave yourselves, both of you. You're mature people, not adolescents in the throes of your first love-affair!'

Unabashed, they traded a small private smile before Saul transferred his gaze to her. 'Do you want a rose named after you?'

Stephanie's red-bronze head tilted. 'It would be a lovely way to be remembered,' she said doubtfully. 'He says that it's a seedling hybrid tea with a scent like no other rose he's ever smelt. Which could mean it's vile, of course.'

Candace put down her piece of toast. 'Don't be so cynical,' she commanded. 'I can cope with it in your brother, but I'm damned if I'm going to listen to it from you.'

Sometimes Candace's transparent honesty and open, delighted appreciation of life grated painfully, and before Stephanie could stop herself she said on a lightly mocking note, 'Goes with the territory, darling. Too much money, too much power—bad for the character, you know. You were lucky, growing up in your foster homes. At least you never had anyone butter you up because your brother was one of the richest men in the world.'

'That's enough,' Saul said, the smooth note in his deep voice an unnecessary warning.

'Don't take any notice of me,' Stephanie said immediately and penitently. 'I'm a pig, and I got out of bed on the wrong side this morning.'

After a narrow glance Saul went back to his newspaper while Candace observed with a trace of acid, 'I wish you'd both stop treating me as though I'm some delicate little butterfly carrying her illusions around like a banner. I'll have you know that I was looking after myself more than capably by the time I was eighteen. Furthermore, pregnancy does not turn your brain to whipped cream and your feelings to slush!'

Saul's hard face softened fractionally as he looked at her. 'Neither Stephanie nor I think you're stupid and over-emotional,' he said.

'Never,' Stephanie agreed promptly, more than a little guilty at precipitating this. Candace had sailed through her first two pregnancies but this one, five years after the second, was being more of a trial. 'You're bright, you're tough, you run our lives with flair and charm and love, you can intimidate strong men if you want to, and your family adores you. As well, you have the crustiest gardeners on every estate eating out of your pretty little hand, even when you decide to change shrub borders that have been in place for a couple of hundred years. What more do you want, you greedy wench?'

Candace said solemnly, 'Respect.'

'Respect?' Saul sighed. 'Dear God, woman, you're insatiable. You really will have to take some advice about setting your sights too high, you know.'

And that, thought Stephanie, listening to her sister's delighted gurgle of laughter, was what the matter with her was. No one could live with Candace and Saul and not realise how hopelessly, utterly in love the two of them were. In their world, as Stephanie knew well, such love was a rare thing.

In the very newspaper that Saul had put down were discreet headlines detailing the messy break-up of yet another marriage among the rich and famous. Stephanie remembered a woman who had been three years ahead of her at school, a brilliant student and then a radiant bride. She had envied Imogen her fairy-tale marriage yet apparently it had been hollow almost from the day after the huge society wedding.

Love, the kind she wanted, the only kind she would settle for, didn't seem to last in their hothouse circle. Except for Saul and Candace. Even for them there had been tense moments; there were always rumours, and several women in the gutter press had insinuated that they had slept with Saul. Not recently, however; for himself Saul didn't care, but he did for Candace, and the resultant court cases had been prompt, savage, and successful.

Wondering forlornly whether she was going to drift through the rest of her life trying to find the same sort of love, Stephanie looked back at her letter. 'I rather like the idea of having a rose named after me,' she said contemplatively. 'When I wander round the garden at home and listen to Peter talking about Madame Georges Bruant—"she's looking lovely this year; always a good doer, is Madame, although a bit coarse, mind you, for real good looks"—well, I don't know anything about the real Madame Bruant, but her name lingers on and gives me enormous pleasure. Yes, I'll tell him he can do it. Of course, I want to see the rose first.' She glanced up at the address. 'Oh, he lives close to Auckland,' she said. 'I can fly down and do some shopping, see the rose, and come back the next day. Do you want anything from Auckland, Candace?'

Her sister's gaze travelled across a lawn green and lush as they could only be in the tropics, over a bank of trees that positively vibrated with life and fecundity, and on to a lagoon glowing with the colours of a black opal. Greens and blues so deep and intense that they hurt the eyes contrasted with areas of milky opalescence, the gleam of scarlet and crimson saved for the evening when the brief tropical sunset drenched everything in saturated colour. Two children played beneath the shade of a mango tree, chattering in the local Maori language to each other. Holidays at Fala'isi had given both Angharad and Matthew a good working knowledge of the island tongue, a knowledge now being honed by their temporary attendance at the school down the road.

'No,' Candace said simply, transferring her eyes back to the austerely splendid structure of her husband's face. 'Not a single thing.'

A truly happy woman. Sometimes Stephanie found herself wondering if that transparent happiness was merely a cover for less attractive emotions, if beneath it there lurked dislike and growing irritation and the taking-for-granted boredom she had seen so often in other faces.

No, if she started suspecting Candace and Saul she might as well give up and try to lose herself in drugs as others of her privileged set had done, risking everything for the deceitful promise of chemicals.

So she wouldn't worry about them, and she wouldn't look at every marriage as though it might be rotten at the core and ready to break; she'd stop being cynical.

In the meantime there was this business of a rose...

'You'd better give me his address,' Saul said, folding his paper and rising. 'I'll get someone to check it out.'

Wordlessly Stephanie handed over the letter. She knew the rules, none better. Adam Cowdray and his background would be pried into, examined by experts in their murky field, and if anything in the least suspicious turned up there would be no meeting.

Some hours later, still wet from a swim, she paused on her way back to the house beside the only rose that seemed to grow on the island, a small, raspberry-flowered scrambler, and gently touched the warm of the petals.

A flower-breeder, she thought. What a blissful, calm, tranquil career. To spend your life in a garden... She lifted the rose to her face, and inhaled the faint, delicate, unmistakable perfume.

'You're looking pensive,' Candace commented from her lounger in the thick shade of the mango tree. She was embroidering tiny yellow rosebuds on a tiny cream dress. 'Are you getting bored?'

Stephanie sighed elaborately. They had been over this before. 'No, I could never get bored on Fala'isi, and yes, I like being here with you, and with faxes and telephones I can conduct all my business just as well as if I were in London. It should be better, because here we're twelve hours ahead of London, but Saul says that's a fallacy!' She settled the thin twig back into the bush. 'I was just deciding what a rose-grower would be like,' she explained. 'Earthy, I think, yet not too much, because roses are rich and intense.'

Candace moved her bulky figure into a more comfortable position, her dark grey gaze steady and a little speculative. 'Ruthless,' she offered, and when Stephanie looked startled, 'I believe that for every seedling that's worth growing on you have to throw out hundreds, possibly thousands. And he'd need to be patient, too, as well as dextrous.'

'Dextrous?'

'Someone has to fertilise the blossoms,' she explained. 'You can't just hope for a stray bee to do the job, you know. Intelligent, too, to understand the genetics. And you will never know how much I've enjoyed your company here these last few months.'

'Well, it's a terrible sacrifice to give up the scintillating weather of a London autumn for the dreariness of a South Sea island, but virtue is its own reward, they say. No more about it, all right? He'd need to be practical.' Stephanie wandered across to the other lounger and lowered herself into it. 'A good businessman.'

'Reliable, because of the records he'd have to keep, with a dash of the visionary thrown in. And tough.'

Stephanie yawned. 'Tough? Come on now, all that would happen to him would be a few scratches from roses reluctant to give up their pollen for the greater good of rosekind.'

'Don't forget those almost-winners he'd have to discard. Anyway, I've met him, and if ever a man is tough Adam Cowdray is that man. I wonder whether he could be tender too?' Candace pondered this thought, then laughed softly. 'All in all an intriguing character. I'll be interested to see what you think of him.'

'I don't know that I really want to go, but I'm not having the man put out an inferior product in my name.'

'Sometimes,' her sister observed, 'you remind me very much of your brother.'

'He almost brought me up so I suppose some of his attitudes have rubbed off on me.'

'Most of them, I'd say.' Her sister's voice was dry. 'But he did a good job. Still waiting, Steph?'

Before she could stop the small, betraying movement Stephanie turned her head away so that her sister's eyes couldn't see beyond the fall of her hair and the curve of her cheek.

'No,' she said lightly. 'Another thing Saul taught me was never to hanker after lost causes.'

'When you arrived on our doorstep that night I could have killed the man who had done that to you, but—you were only eighteen, love, barely more than a child. No one blamed you for falling for him. He sounded an immensely charismatic man, and he'd cared for you.'

'He was a criminal.' The ugly, uncompromising word hung in the balmy air. Levelly she resumed, 'He tried to kill me.'

'Did he? I've often wondered.'

'I felt the bullets whistle past,' Stephanie said.

'Yes, but have you ever wondered why, if he was that close, he didn't hit you?'

Of course she had, and sometimes she had even allowed herself to hope that he had deliberately missed her. But only a few months ago she had forced herself to face the truth. For the last five years she had been in love with a figment of her imagination, and it was time she stopped it, gave up the lingering miasma of the past.

'Perhaps,' Candace finished, 'he was trying to save you.'

Stephanie smiled obliquely. 'Oh, over the years I've come up with a whole variety of reasons for him to be helping the men who kidnapped me, but none of them fits. He was in it for the money and I was expendable. He did try to kill me. He didn't manage it because I was running like hell, and it was dark. And handguns are not particularly accurate.'

If he'd been caught and put on trial she'd have seen him for what he was, instead of harbouring pathetic hopes that he was some sort of Scarlet Pimpernel figure playing a dangerous double game. It would have been over, and she'd have been able to get on with her life. Instead he'd disappeared as irrevocably as the men who had kidnapped her. Nothing had ever been heard of them again.

Candace persisted, 'Yet he took you out of that horrible crypt. Why did he do that?'

'I think I was only left there to calm me down and make me trust him. They couldn't kill me because obviously Saul needed to know that I was still alive.' It hurt to say it, to remember how naïvely gullible she'd been. 'He knew that if he was kind to me I wouldn't believe that he was one of them.'

Candace frowned. 'Logically it makes sense, but I don't believe you would have been so easily fooled. I've always felt that you have a really good understanding of character. If you fell in love with him——'

'It's called the Stockholm syndrome,' Stephanie interrupted. 'And it's a protective mechanism. Hostages identify with their abductors because it seems the only road to survival.'

'I know.' But Candace persevered, 'All the same, I think there must have been some good in him or you wouldn't have fallen so hard. Oh, women do love criminals, but most of them know damned well they're fools. And you've never been quite convinced, have you?'

She saw too much. For five years Stephanie had tried to persuade herself that Duke was evil, and for five years her emotions had warred with logic.

'Oh, yes, I'm sure. Don't forget poor Halliday. Duke almost killed him.'

'He knocked him out.'

Stephanie said brusquely, 'It was just sheer good luck he wasn't killed. If the blow had been a little harder— it's usually fatal, that chop to the throat.'

'Funny about that,' Candace said. 'Halliday disappeared shortly after that, did you know?'

'No. What's funny about it?'

'Well, he just vanished,' Candace said vaguely. 'And hasn't it ever occurred to you that Duke couldn't manage to hit you when he fired at you, and he didn't kill Halliday, yet everything you've said about him makes him sound like a man who doesn't make mistakes?'

'On the contrary, he made several,' Stephanie said angrily.

'Do you think that he could kill anyone in cold blood?'

Stephanie bit her lip. 'Oh, yes,' she said with remote composure. 'I heard him discuss it, and believe me, he was not philosophically opposed to the taking of life. Of course, he didn't much like killing women, but he was going to make himself smother me. I just wish I could get rid of him,' she cried passionately. 'He made a total and complete fool of me, but however hard I try I can't get him out of my head! Not even by——'

'Not even by falling in love with someone else?'

Stephanie grimaced. 'Not even by falling in love with someone else. Because I did love Philip.' As always when speaking of the man she had planned to marry, her voice took on a defensive note. 'Only...'

Candace supplied the answer she couldn't. 'Only you couldn't go to bed with him. And you could with Duke.'

'I didn't go to bed with Duke. I quite deliberately set out to seduce him so that I could betray him.'

Candace said quietly, 'You did what you had to do to survive. Don't you think it's time to stop punishing yourself because you enjoyed seducing him and wanted to make love properly? You were very young, and very inexperienced...'

'Perhaps I should have slept with him.' Stephanie had never spoken to Candace with such frankness before. In a way, it was desperation, because Duke was still embedded in her life like grit in tar, so deeply established in some rebellious corner of her heart that she didn't seem to be able to free herself from the sinister clutches of her obsession. She said moodily, 'If I had, I might have got him out of my system.'

'Perhaps. You're not ever going to know, and that's what you have to accept. Sometimes in life things don't get resolved. The whole experience was horrifying, and you've come out of it remarkably well, because you were very vulnerable,' Candace said astutely, adding with a shiver, 'Saul wanted to kill him. I was very glad he dis-

appeared so completely. I didn't mind him being dead,
but I did not want Saul to go to prison for doing it.'

Stephanie shivered a little. Her brother had some extremely uncivilised responses. 'Let's hope he's mod-
erated his attitudes by the time Angharad grows up.'

'I think it was because he felt so powerless. He's not
accustomed to not being able to do anything. As for
Angharad, I've no doubt she'll make him see sense,'
Candace said placidly.

Both women grinned, for Saul's daughter was as
strong-willed as he.

'What's it like living with someone as tough as Saul?'

'You should know, you've lived with him almost all
your life.' But Candace smiled, and her voice altered as
it always did when she spoke or thought of her husband.
'It's not easy, but then, I didn't expect it to be. He doesn't
find it easy to live with me, either. Loving someone is
difficult; it gives you strength, but it weakens you too.
You've delivered a hostage to fortune. I don't think I'm
neurotic but occasionally I wonder what my life would
be like if fortune behaved cruelly. Because I know there
will never be another love for me like that. Saul is an
impossible act to follow.'

Oh, yes, an impossible act.

Yet once Stephanie had been sure she'd discovered a
man who measured up to Saul, a man who had come
to her in the midst of pain and terror and humiliation
and saved her, faced down her demons and fought
through hell to rescue her.

Childish sentimentality, she thought now, five years
later. At the impressionable age of eighteen, when it was
still possible to believe in heroes and princes on white
chargers, she had been in dire peril. Duke had rescued
her, so she had endowed him with all the noble qualities
she wanted in a mate. Instead, he had betrayed her.

The smile that curled her full mouth was more than
a little ironic. And she had fooled him.

Candace's voice interrupted her unprofitable thoughts. 'But you can't live like that, worrying about the future. All you can do is take each day as it comes and extract the utmost from it. When are you going to Auckland?'

'Tomorrow. I'll stay a couple of nights—there's a suffrage exhibition I'd like to see while I'm there.'

'Will you call anyone? Guy and Mike Lorimer will be at home; Mike's like me, not travelling at the moment. Their baby's due three weeks after this monster here.'

'I'll see them, of course, but I don't want to socialise.' She stretched out languidly and closed her eyes. 'I don't want to spend too much time there—I'm enjoying this too much.'

The biggest Polynesian city in the world, Auckland sprawled across the isthmus between its two harbours, so intricately interwoven with the sea that even in a plane it was impossible to separate one harbour from the other.

Stephanie shivered slightly as she walked the short distance to the car that waited for her. It was the middle month of spring; but although it was fine the temperature was considerably lower than the balmy airs of Fala'isi. Still, she liked Auckland, even with a nippy little easterly wind blowing off the Pacific Ocean.

Once settled at the hotel she rang the number from the letterhead on Adam Cowdray's letter. A feminine voice answered, middle-aged, brisk, efficient.

No, she couldn't speak to Mr Cowdray, he was busy, but if she'd like to leave a message...

'Please tell him that Stephanie Jerrard called,' Stephanie said, and left her number. 'I'm going out now, but I'll be back around four.'

'I'll make sure he gets the message,' the secretary said, a hint of frost in her tones.

Probably thinks I'm chasing him, Stephanie thought wryly as she hung up. Ah, well, if he's half as good-looking and charismatic as Candace says, I just might, too!

Saul's security man rang just as she got in from the exhibition. 'Adam Cowdray seems as clean as a picked bone, but we haven't run a full check on him yet. I suggest you take young Robinson with you when you see him,' he said.

It wasn't a command, but Stephanie knew that she had no chance of getting away without the bodyguard's presence. 'OK,' she said amiably.

She had just put the telephone down when it rang again. It was the secretary, still frosty-voiced, who said, 'Mr Cowdray will meet you at the nursery at ten tomorrow morning. It's at Te Atatu.' After giving an address which Stephanie wrote down, she added, 'Please try not to be late. Mr Cowdray is very busy.'

'I,' Stephanie said pleasantly, 'am always punctual. I'm relying on you to make sure that Mr Cowdray is too. Goodbye.'

And she hung up, rather basely enjoying the startled gasp her comment had caused.

She spent the evening quietly with the Lorimers, coming home early because, like Candace, Mike was finding the last stages of her pregnancy tiring.

As she got her key from the desk she thought wearily that she didn't begrudge her friends and relatives their happiness; she merely found it a bitter irony that she couldn't forget the man who strode like a colossus through her past.

The next day was fine and summery, the air softening with the departure of the wind. Stephanie ran down to the car and, smiling, gave the address to the large man behind the wheel.

'How's your wife and the new baby?' she asked, and spent the drive along the north-western motorway catching up. She had known Brett Robinson for several years, and liked him very much, so she listened to his bashful rendition of the delights of his baby with interest. After three sons he was a doting father to the little girl.

The rose nursery was set behind high conifer hedges down a side-road surrounded by vineyards. A discreet sign announced that it was the Cowdray Rose Nursery. Equally discreet white-painted gates were firmly closed.

'I'll open them,' Stephanie said.

'I'll do it.' Brett Robinson was already halfway out, and for the first time she remembered that he was only half-chauffeur. The rest was bodyguard.

Sighing, she settled down in her seat.

Inside, a white-painted office was set in rose gardens, brilliant with the season's flowers. Some distance away behind another, lower hedge was a house, double-storeyed and sprawling beneath an orange tiled roof. A huge jacaranda tree to one side was budding up, the intense violet tips of the branches hinting at the joyous bounty to come.

It was very still, with no sign of anyone about.

'I'll come with you,' Brett said, looking around keenly.

Stephanie was a little uneasy herself. There seemed to be an unusual waiting quality to the warm silence, a feeling that something was happening, or about to happen. Not, she thought wearily, that that was anything to go by; she had felt perfectly safe walking down the silent street in Switzerland a few seconds before the kidnappers had struck.

Still, she was glad of Brett's large presence beside her as she walked up to the office and opened the door. No one was inside, no frosty-voiced female, no rose-growing hunk.

Brett called out, but no one answered.

'Perhaps I got the time wrong,' Stephanie suggested, knowing very well she hadn't.

Brett said briskly, 'I'll see if I can rustle someone up at the house.'

They were halfway along the path to the house when a woman came around the back hedge and strode towards them. The frosty female, Stephanie decided.

Sure enough, in arctic tones the newcomer said, 'Miss Jerrard?'

'Yes.'

'I'm sorry, but Mr Cowdray has been called away on an emergency.' There was not so much frost as fluster in her voice when she went on, 'He asked if it would be all right to make another appointment for tomorrow.'

'Yes, of course.'

Two minutes later Stephanie was back in the car, wondering what sort of emergency a rose-breeder had. A bee pollinating the wrong flower?

Brett left her at the hotel door, and she had coffee in the elegant coffee-room, watched the people who frequented it with interested eyes, and then went up to her room, deciding to fill in the extra hours with a visit to her favourite spot in Auckland—the Aquarium along the Waterfront Drive. She had just opened the door when a hand fell on her shoulder; she was pushed unceremoniously into the room, and even before she turned she knew who was standing behind her.

His dark face was eagle-featured, strong and uncompromising, from the glittering crystals of his eyes, pale, icy as slivers of quartz, to the scar that ran up the right side of his face from the arrogant jaw to a point just under his eye.

A complex, bewildering mixture of emotions—fear and a wild, singing, unrepentant joy—ran through her, followed fast by anger and the sickening panic she remembered so well.

'Hello, Stephanie,' he said calmly, closing the door behind them both. 'You should always look along the corridor before you open your hotel door.'

The room was very quiet, its restrained opulence in infinite counterpoint to the undiluted masculinity of the man who stood before her. Although she knew she should be yelling at the top of her lungs, pressing the security button, doing anything rather than standing there as though she'd been frozen, she couldn't move.

'D-Duke?' she stammered at last.

'I'm Adam Cowdray,' he said.

'But...'

His smile was sardonic. 'You didn't really think that I'd been christened Duke, did you?'

'What are you doing here?' she asked, eyes stretched so wide that they were painful in her white face.

Duke—Adam—Cowdray's glance was searching. 'I applaud your caution, but I refuse to talk to you with a bodyguard in attendance,' he said.

'You were there,' she whispered. 'At the nursery.'

'Yes.'

She had known. She had recognised his presence—that peculiar, waiting stillness, the feeling of impending doom. Fighting off the suffocating intensity of the emotions churning through her, she asked with a bitter smile, 'Have you come to kidnap me again?'

'I didn't kidnap you last time,' he said curtly. 'If you remember, I rescued you.'

'You were going to kill me. I heard you that last night. "I gave her a knock-out pill to keep her under...it will be easy enough to smother her",' she mimicked bitterly.

'How did you manage to wake up so fast? I expected to have to throw a couple of gallons of cold water over you, then make you drink gallons of black coffee before I got you in a fit state to run for your life.'

'I was sick,' she told him. 'Either a bug or exhaust fumes when we were going through the city. And don't change the subject. You shot at me. Twice.'

'And missed you, twice. Don't try to pretend you're a fool, princess.' The taut mouth closed like a trap on the words. 'If I'd wanted to kill you you'd be dead. You didn't believe it then and you don't believe it now. Look at you—you're not scared, you're bloody furious!'

He was right, damn him.

'You lied to me and betrayed me. You told me you were working for Saul, but he'd never heard of you, didn't even know that I was all right.'

'I got you back to him,' he returned blandly. 'He may not have known that I was working for him, but I was.'

Rage, bushfire-fierce, all-consuming, rose like bile within her. She reined it in, because if she gave way to it now she'd try to kill him. And that, she knew, was impossible.

'I got myself back,' she snapped.

'Come off it, Stephanie. Do you honestly think I didn't know what you'd planned? As soon as I came up the stairs and saw you there I was almost certain you must have overheard what we were saying. The toothbrush was a pretty good indication too, as was your amusing imitation of a woman who wanted nothing more than sex, quick and hot and heavy. I knew for certain when you flicked the keys from my pocket. Actually, I was quite proud of you. You kept your head and used the only weapon you had, and you chose exactly the right moment to do it.' He smiled at her astonished, affronted face. 'Which, princess, was why your knee in my groin didn't have quite the expected effect. I knew the exact moment you gathered yourself to do it and managed to take avoiding action.'

'If you knew, why did you let me go on making a fool of myself?'

His eyes were colourless beneath his black lashes, as unreadable as his expression. 'It was as good a way as any I could think of to get you out of there and still keep my credibility with the rest of them,' he said coolly. 'It worked, too. Just. We agreed that you must have overheard the conversation I had with Benny, and of course none of them blamed me for accepting your offer of sex, especially as I thought I had plenty of time. They even considered I'd done quite well to get myself off the bed so quickly after you'd kneed me. Pity I hadn't managed to kill you, but, as we decided afterwards, it wasn't absolutely necessary. Actually, it was Sounder's idea. He hadn't bothered to clear it with the bosses.'

Dragging her eyes free of his mesmeric gaze, Stephanie shook her head. 'So you're not a murderer,' she said coolly. 'Big deal.' She swallowed to ease a rasping dryness in her throat. 'What do you want now? Another go at twenty million pounds?'

'Don't be a fool, Stephanie. I want you to listen to me.'

She gave him a scathing look and took another small step backwards. 'I have to. I can't throw you out.'

He showed perfect teeth in a smile as humourless and callous as granite, walked over to the telephone table and picked up the inconspicuous electronic device she would have had around her neck if Brett hadn't been with her that morning.

Duke's—Adam's—long, tanned fingers looked capable and strong as he held it out to her. 'Use it,' he said. 'Or ring through to the switchboard here. The hotel will send someone up if you really want to get rid of me.'

She looked at the device, then slowly raised her eyes to his. Beneath his thick lashes they blazed, light refracted in ice. He was smiling, but there was no humour in it. She knew her face reflected her tormented uncertainty, because he said softly, 'Your decision, princess.'

'You don't know what you're asking,' she said bleakly.

'I'm asking you to listen, that's all. I realise it's a hell of a step for you to take, especially as you've spent the last five years thinking of me as a criminal of the worst sort.'

Don't, common sense shrieked. You trusted him once before, and look what happened; you fell in love, and you have never got over it.

She looked up, into eyes colder and more distant than polar seas. He wasn't going to help her; he'd made no promises, given her no excuses.

'All right,' she said in a muted voice, thinking, you fool, oh, you fool!

Nothing altered in the scarred warrior's face. 'Sit down,' he said. 'Can I get you a drink?'

'No!'

But she sat down, collapsing with more speed than grace on to the sofa. He sat down too, looking oddly at home in the muted luxury of the room, dominating it effortlessly.

Now that she had taken the plunge she didn't want to hear what he had to say; telling herself that she needed time to collect her thoughts, she asked, 'What are you doing growing roses in Auckland?'

'It's the family business,' Duke—Adam—said.

She nodded. 'Candace said it was an old firm.'

Without inflexion he told her, 'My grandfather set it up as a hobby at first, then, when he became obsessed with it, as a business. My father followed him.'

Feeling as though she had walked into *Alice in Wonderland*, Stephanie looked around the quiet room, similar to a hundred other hotel rooms she'd been in, attractive, soothing, impersonal, but not so impersonal as the man who sat opposite her.

'Have you come to tell me that you agree to my naming a rose after you?' he asked, apparently, like her, in no hurry.

'I want to see it first,' she said, fighting to overcome the odd, frightened hysteria that threatened to clog her throat.

'Naturally. I thought I could donate the profits to some sort of charity. One of your choosing, of course.'

She realised anew how very intimidating he could be. There was something overwhelming about him, an uncompromising aura of force and authority found in few men. Saul had it; and that, she thought, trying to be objective, had to be one of the reasons she had fallen so hard for Duke.

Because although he didn't have Saul's money, or the sort of power Saul could call on, Duke—Adam—had the same effortless, unfaltering impact. Dazed and traumatised though she had been when she had first met him, she had recognised that controlled strength and responded helplessly to it.

'Yes, I'd like that,' she said. 'The Save the Children Foundation. If it's going to make lots, why don't we divide it up and send some to the Fred Hollowes Fund? The Third World could do with some more factories making optical lenses.'

The sun through the window beat on to his head, coaxing a blue sheen from his hair, gilding his olive skin. The aquiline nose and square chin were separate statements of ruthlessness. He looked older—all of his thirty years.

Dangerous, criminal, a man with no softness, yet something blind and passionate stirred and stretched inside her.

'So tell me,' she said crisply, before that weakness could conquer her better judgement, 'what you were doing in Switzerland five years ago.'

He leaned back in his chair and looked at her from beneath his lashes. 'I was trying to infiltrate a criminal gang that was organising the stealing of nuclear weapons from Russia in order to smuggle them at exorbitant profit to organisations and countries I won't name.'

It was nothing like she had expected. Fighting her instinctive need to believe, she said acidly, 'And where did I fit into that?'

'You,' he said deliberately, 'were the cash cow. They needed money to pay their contacts in Russia, and Saul Jerrard was an obvious target. When I finally got an entry into the group they'd just kidnapped you. I managed to convince them that you were better out of that crypt and in my care.' His smile was cold and predatory. 'Looked at from their point of view, it was a good move. If anyone managed to track you down, I'd be the fall guy.'

'So the man who came to see you at the castle was one of them.'

'Yes. Your brother wasn't in any great hurry to pay over the ransom, probably believing that if he did it could sign your death warrant. His security division had done some damned fine work and got too close, and as things weren't nearly ready for the ransom drop we had to move out of the castle before he could rescue you.'

'How did you know they were closing in?' she asked swiftly. 'I can't imagine they were exactly obvious.'

'Someone allowed himself to be heard asking questions in the village.'

'Who?' she demanded.

'Halliday.' His smile was pure irony. 'Didn't you guess? I thought you might; your brother certainly did, which was why Halliday suddenly disappeared. He was my contact in your brother's organisation.'

'Halliday was a criminal?' She shook her head. 'But you tried to kill him.'

'I tried very hard not to kill him,' he returned laconically. 'I hit him hard enough to look good and take the pressure off him. And no, neither Halliday nor I was a criminal.'

She swallowed. 'Who were you both working for?'

'I can't tell you that, but it was a British-based undercover organisation. Barely official. We did the real dirty work.'

She said thinly, 'Does Saul know this?'

'Saul knows that Halliday was as clean as any of us. I doubt if my name ever appeared in the consultations he had with some of my bosses when the five million pounds he did finally pay over was refunded.' He smiled grimly. 'I believe he scorched their ears and told them in no uncertain terms that if any of his family was made use of again like that he'd see that heads rolled. And as he has the power to do it they were suitably chastened.'

Stephanie said, 'Go on. Saul's money was necessary to the gang, and it was necessary for you to let them get it. So they moved us on to the chalet. I don't suppose the castle had been bugged.'

'No. That was another convenient lie.'

'I was a complete idiot,' she said stonily.

He shrugged. 'Why shouldn't you believe me? We went to a lot of trouble to make my story hang together. And the fact that I'd rescued you made it quite easy for you to trust me.'

She showed her teeth. 'Not entirely.'

'No.' He smiled. 'You might have been a little naïve, but you weren't stupid.'

She glowered at him, but the forceful countenance revealed nothing. Losing her composure wasn't going to get her anywhere; she took a deep breath. 'All right, go on.'

'I thought you might have got over that arrogance,' he said mildly, not attempting to hide the diamond glitter in his eyes. 'Too much to expect, I suppose. Anyway, then Sounder sprang his little surprise; he decided that I should kill you.'

She said, 'Wasn't that intended right from the start?'

'It was always on the cards, of course, but they had a pretty good idea of the sort of hornets' nest they'd bring about their ears if they did. No, that was Sounder's little scheme. You'd seen his face—which, incidentally, was something you didn't tell me—but, more than that, he was suspicious of me.'

'I didn't tell you,' she said, 'because I wasn't entirely taken in by your lies. I was pretty sure that you were telling me the truth, but I had some confused idea that if you weren't and I did tell you I could well be signing my death warrant. I wasn't thinking too clearly at the time. Anyway, what good would it have done?'

'I could have made some contingency plans,' he said caustically, 'instead of having the whole thing dumped in my lap at the last moment. As it happens, your seeing his face was only an excuse; they wanted a hold over me and murdering you would have given them the best. So they sent Benny in to tell me to do it, and taped the conversation so they'd be able to use it against me.'

'How do you know all this?'

'I found out,' he said. 'That's what I was good at—collecting information.'

He was taking the past and turning it on his head, and she wanted—oh, how she wanted—to trust him. But it wasn't going to be so easy. 'Would you have killed me?'

'You know the answer to that. I had the chance,' he said without hesitation or expression. 'I was prepared to do almost anything else, because infiltrating this group was important; if those nuclear weapons got through, a lot of innocent people would have died. However, I drew the line at killing anyone to get there.'

She bit her lip. 'How were you planning to get out of it?'

'I didn't dare break cover; too much was riding on my staying in the group.'

'And you didn't trust me to keep quiet.'

He said crisply, 'You were going to be interrogated by experts, and we did not want anyone to know what we were doing in case word found its way back to the group, some of whom had ties with the murky world we all worked in. I contacted Halliday and we decided to engineer a rescue. He was going to come in with guns blazing, shoot me in the arm and gallantly rescue you. Not particularly brilliant, but it could have worked. Then you made your charming attempt at seduction, and that was an even better idea.'

'Why?'

He showed his teeth in a formidable smile. 'Because you initiated it, and you'd be interrogated by men who would understand just how tempting an offer like that would be to an unprincipled cad.' His tone was subtly mocking as he said the last three words.

'I see.'

'Unfortunately,' he went on, 'we hadn't planned on Benny keeping close watch. He let off a couple of shots at you as you hared off down the road, so I had to get you out of his way and make it seem as though I was trying to shoot you in the woods. They didn't really care whether you were dead or not, as long as they had the tape of me saying I'd kill you. Amusing, because the last thing I intended to do was let them toss me out. Anyway, it all worked out well enough. They decided the five million pounds they'd collected in England the night you got away would have to do, and my cover was still unblown.'

'So I played completely into your hands.'

'You did, princess.'

She could have bridled at the hated nickname, but she was too humiliated to make the effort. She said, 'What happened after that?'

'I can't tell you, but the men who tried to smuggle out the bombs and missiles are now either dead or so far behind bars, they aren't coming out again.'

'So what you're saying is that there's no way anyone can find out whether what you've told me is the truth or not,' she said slowly.

His lashes drooped further. 'Unless you want to visit several gaols in the less salubrious parts of the world, that's about it,' he said indifferently.

Did she believe him? Taken all in all, she thought she did. He might have been lying, but unless he had killed the real Adam Cowdray he was almost certainly who he said he was.

That didn't, of course, mean that he wasn't a criminal. At the very least he had used her callously. But his story reconciled the two sides of his character, the perverse dichotomy that had so bewildered her: the man who had cared for her and the one who had casually talked about killing her.

Perhaps Candace had been right.

And perhaps not.

Because what decision she came to didn't really alter anything. While she had been falling in love he had seen her as a commodity, a pawn to be sacrificed for the greatest advantage. Possibly he'd had the welfare of the world at heart, but he certainly hadn't cared about hers. She had been a means to an end, discarded with no thought when her usefulness was over.

'Why have you contacted me now?' she asked at last.

Something evanescent and dangerous gleamed in those unusual eyes. 'Perhaps I wanted to see how you'd turned out,' he said smoothly.

'I'm not much different,' she returned every bit as smoothly. 'A few years older, that's all, and probably more than a little bit wiser. A person's basic character doesn't change much.'

His brows lifted. 'So you're still the pretty innocent of five years ago.'

She said drily, 'I don't know that innocence is a part of one's character. Of course I'm not so guileless—I spent four of those years at university.'

'Doing what?'

'A business management degree,' she said, refusing to look at him. 'But that's not particularly interesting. Why have you told me all this now?'

'Because it's time you knew the truth. The men who kidnapped you are both dead.'

She stared at him in horror. 'Did you kill them?' And she knew even before his mouth twisted that he wasn't going to answer.

But he did.

CHAPTER SEVEN

'No.' Duke looked directly at her, pupils dark as midnight, ice-rimmed. 'They died in a shoot-out. However, I was instrumental in making sure they ended up like rats in a cage. I set the trap, and I baited it, and I'm not in the least sorry they decided to shoot it out rather than surrender.'

A weight Stephanie didn't even know she'd been carrying rolled free. She hadn't realised how much difference it would make. 'I shouldn't be pleased they're dead,' she said quietly, 'but—I used to dream that they came back for me. Thank you for telling me.'

'They were no loss to humanity, believe me. They'd have killed you without a qualm if it had suited them to.' That cold smile narrowed. 'You were a victim in someone else's war. I thought you needed to know that they were no longer a threat.' His hooded eyes were unreadable, the strong, harsh lines of his face closed against her.

A small, bittersweet smile tilted the corners of her mouth but she said nothing. What else had she expected? That he had contacted her because he had been wildly, obsessively, passionately in love with her for the last five years? Grow up, Stephanie. That's not how the world works.

He went on, 'No one can recompense you for what you endured, but I can name a rose after you. It's no restitution of what we took from you, but it's the best I can do.'

'I see,' she said slowly. 'When can I see it?'

'May I use your telephone?'

She nodded, and watched him get to his feet and walk across to the table. It was difficult to reconcile the man she had known five years ago with this man, seemingly content to breed flowers.

Oh, physically he hadn't changed much; he still moved with the swift, noiseless grace that she had seen so often in the tangle of her dreams. Although he was young enough for his blue-black hair to show no strand of grey, the lines that bracketed his mouth were a little more deeply engraved. The scar hadn't aged him; it merely emphasised the edged, dangerous look that had kept her so off-balance five years before. And the potent, blazing aura of sexuality was just as elemental as before.

He didn't look at her as he rang Reception and ordered the roses he'd left there to be brought up, yet Stephanie felt him in every cell of her body, an itch in her blood she had never been able to soothe.

As he put the receiver down she got to her feet, unable to cope with a silence filled by the aching poignancy of her memories. 'Excuse me,' she said, 'I'll be back in a minute,' and fled into her bedroom. In the bathroom she washed her face and let the cool water play over her wrists until she heard the doorbell.

'I'll get it,' Duke said.

From the bedroom door she watched as he went across to the door, noting that he opened it with caution although he didn't check the peephole. Something pulled at her heart.

It was, however, the bellboy with a vase of flowers, a great mass of red-bronze petals with a perfume that floated like incense across the room.

Stephanie made a sound of appreciation.

'See if you like the scent,' Duke—Adam—said, putting them down on the coffee-table.

Obediently she bent to smell the blooms. Rich but not heavy, an intriguing blend of true rose with a faint hint of something else—the citrus tang of freesias?

'How could I not?' she murmured, lost in an evocative haze.

She sniffed again, and a lean hand reached out, twisted a bloom free and held it against her hair. 'Yes, I thought I had it right,' he said.

She kept her lashes lowered. 'They're lovely,' she said simply.

'Not quite the common thing,' he replied, an ironic note shaping his voice as he handed her the rose.

Stephanie looked up sharply, her eyes lingering compulsively on the scar that marred the arrogant angle of his cheek. 'What happened?' she heard her voice say, stroking the rose petals because her fingers longed to trace the jagged line.

'I had a difference of opinion with a sword,' he said laconically.

Something painful broke, shattered into tiny shards deep inside her.

Dragging her eyes away from his face, she focused on the flower that glowed in her hand, saying with a note of light amusement, 'Thank you for this; it was a nice thought. Creative, too. I rather fancy the idea of having a rose named after me, but if it's exposure you want Candace would be the better bet. She's already being written about as a great innovator.'

'I might ask her one day,' he said, his voice telling her nothing. 'But this one is yours.'

She smiled, smelled the rose again, and said, 'I'd be honoured to sponsor it. Thank you, Duke.'

'Then you had better sign a release,' he said. 'And my name is Adam.'

'Who gave you the nickname?' she asked.

Impatience edged his tone. 'It was just somebody's idea of a joke.'

She gave him a swift sideways look. He might think it a joke, but she didn't; she understood why that unknown person had thought Duke suited him. He carried himself with an air of unconscious self-confidence, a natural aristocrat, looking down from his great height at lesser beings. Arrogant, yes, profoundly irritating certainly, but those characteristics were inborn.

'If you can give me the release, I'll get a lawyer to check it out,' she said, 'and post it to you.'

'I have it here,' he said, taking a paper from his pocket. 'Get him to do it today and you can give it to me tonight. I'll take you out to dinner.'

Anger sparked inside her; yes, arrogance was definitely the word.

'I'm sorry,' she said calmly, 'but that's not possible.'

'How about if I *ask* you to dinner?' Adam said shrewdly.

She knew she shouldn't—she still didn't know whether she really believed him. And yet if she went out to dinner with him she'd be proving that he no longer affected her.

'That's different,' she returned.

'I'll pick you up at seven-thirty.'

It was still an order, but she said slowly, 'All right.'

The minute the door closed behind him she rang London and asked for the man who ran Saul's security. Yawning, because it was the middle of the night there, he answered. After a heartfelt apology, she spoke to him for five minutes, and hung up. Five hours later he rang back.

'What do you think I am, a miracle-worker?' he grumbled, but he'd enjoyed the hunt; she could tell by the tone of his voice. 'These are dangerous waters I've been fishing in. I'll have a few words to say to young Dave. What he got for you was the nicely sanitised version of Adam Cowdray's life in the British Army, and the idiot didn't think to dig any deeper.'

Stephanie realised that her knuckles were turning white. 'Was he in the army?'

'Oh, yes. SAS. I had to call in a few old favours, and apply quite a lot of pressure, and even then they weren't very forthcoming, but a couple of years after he'd done his training he was picked to go into a very covert agency.'

Stephanie dragged in a painful breath. The army had turned him into a warrior, case-hardened him, made him a killing machine.

Apparently unaware of her response, the man in London said, 'I couldn't find out what he'd been doing but he's clean. He resigned four years ago, did a couple of private jobs——'

'What?'

'Oh, the usual. Legal but expensive jobs involving the possibility of violence. You can earn a lot in a short time if you're clever and not particularly concerned about dying.' While she thought this over he asked, 'Did he say what agency he worked for?'

'No. Not a word.'

He gave a grunt of approval. 'Staunch, but then, that's the man. He's been out of circulation here for about six years.'

Two years during undercover, and then the last four years spent breeding roses. Yes, it hung together. 'So I can trust him.'

'I'd trust him with my life,' he said carefully, 'and my wallet, but if I were a woman—well, I don't know. According to my envious informant, at one time he used to have to swat women off him. He had a reputation for being cold-blooded but that didn't seem to worry the females who went after him.'

After another apology for having kept him up half the night, Stephanie put the receiver down with something like relief.

For the past five years she had been unable to trust her own heart when it came to men; she had erred so badly in judging Duke that she had chosen his very antithesis in Philip. And when that hadn't worked out she hadn't dared try again. But the inner promptings of her heart had been right; oh, he had used her, and no doubt she meant nothing to him beyond a woman he had treated badly, but at least he wasn't the criminal she'd thought him to be. She didn't have to despise herself any longer.

Was that why he had contacted her again?

No. He was a hard man. He probably had no idea what he had done to her five years ago.

She wouldn't fall into the trap of endowing him with qualities he didn't have, just to comfort her romantic soul. But now she knew he hadn't lied to her there was no reason why she shouldn't enjoy the evening out with him, and try to lay the ghosts of the past.

She'd packed nothing but a very plain dress, and she didn't know just how much money he could afford to spend. She had no idea whether breeding roses was profitable or not, although presumably he had bankrolled himself by the private jobs he had undertaken, those legal but dangerous positions where it helped not to worry about the possibility of death. The thought of them made her feel sick.

So she wore her plain dress, a silk shirtwaister in her favourite shades of autumn, and deliberately left her hair in its usual curly unset style, wearing only the pearl studs Saul had given her for her twentieth birthday. The fabulous teardrops, faintly gleaming with a pale gold sheen that harmonised so well against her ivory skin, were treasures from Fala'isi's warm lagoon.

Wondering what differences Adam saw, she gazed at her reflection. In Switzerland she had been thin, her skin sallow and rough and patchy with fear and confinement, her hair lank and unkempt in spite of the constant washing she had indulged in. Now her skin glowed with the creamy matt finish that photographed so well, and her eyes were a glittering, audacious blue. Colour crackled through her hair; she turned her head in a consciously preening gesture, then made a derisory face at herself.

She was an idiot.

Ready ten minutes early, she sat down in her room and gazed blindly out over Auckland's waterfront, hands linked tensely in her lap. It was starting all over again; she could feel that hopeless, mindless hunger curling through her veins now.

Remember, he's no prince on a white charger, she told herself impatiently.

All right, so he lied to you, the small, unregenerately hopeful part of her brain argued. He had to. And he's made contact now. That must mean something.

It could mean he's cashing in on the name, she thought cynically. Although that didn't really make sense. Gardeners wouldn't buy a substandard rose simply because it carried the magical Jerrard name—he had to know that many of them wouldn't know who the Jerrards were, and couldn't care less.

She tried to dam the rising tide of excitement and anticipation because it made her far too vulnerable. She wasn't the girl of eighteen who had fallen in love with her rescuer; she was five years older, a mature woman who had been engaged, who had taken a degree in business management, who ran her own affairs.

Yet she had a lot in common with that naïve girl. To begin with, she was still a virgin, with a virgin's instinctive fear of the intensity of her emotions. Going out for the evening with the only man who was able to make her feel like this was the most dangerous thing she'd done in the past five years. The fact that Adam's power over her was solely physical, something to do with genes and conditioning, didn't make it any easier to deal with.

When the telephone rang she jumped, only lifting it after the fourth summons. 'Ah, Ms Jerrard, you are there,' the receptionist said pleasantly. 'I'll tell Mr Cowdray that he can come up.'

'No, I'll come down.'

Dressed in the starkness of dinner-jacket and white shirt, Adam dominated the large, marble-lined, fountain-murmuring foyer.

Those clothes, Stephanie thought warily as she paused a moment outside the lift doors, had been tailored especially for that long, heavily muscled body, their elegant, spare sophistication somehow emphasising the unconcealed toughness of the man who wore them. Adam Cowdray was more than a little uncivilised, his steel-reinforced core too close to the surface to be hidden. Once a warrior, it seemed, always a warrior.

The autocratic, high-held head turned, and she felt the full effect of his eyes, their cutting intensity still probing for weaknesses.

Conscious of the covert glances of others, Stephanie pinned a smooth, cool smile to her lips and moved out to greet him. Her breath caught in her lungs; lord, but he was big! He overwhelmed her, made her knees tremble and her belly clench in a primitive, feverish response.

She held out her hand, keeping it steady by an effort of will. Of course she expected him to shake it; she was astonished and not a little confused when he raised it and kissed her knuckles.

'Heavens!' she said, irritated by the slight but definite recoil that must have given her away. 'No one does that now, Du—Adam, unless it's middle-aged European aristocrats saluting the hands of elderly dowagers!'

'I make my own rules,' he said, something untamed glinting in the depths of his eyes.

Oh, yes, he made his own rules. And if people got hurt, that was their bad luck.

He'd left his car underneath the hotel portico; to Stephanie's surprise, the doorman greeted him by name as he opened the door for her.

Still, why should she be surprised? He stood out; his very size made him easily recognisable. Wondering how he had managed to be a good secret agent when he was such a commanding, authoritative figure, she settled back into the car and looked out at the pleasant Auckland street, angling her jaw purposefully. Five years ago he'd held all the cards in his spare, graceful hands; this time she would maintain her autonomy and reclaim her self-respect.

He took her to a restaurant that was small, secluded and family-run, where he was also greeted by name. As they sat with the menu, she said, 'Tell me how an intrepid agent turned into a rose-breeder.'

'My father was dying,' he said, his voice aloof, his eyes never leaving hers. 'I knew that more than anything he wanted me to keep on with the roses, and I knew that he wouldn't say a word about it.'

'Did he approve of your life rescuing maidens and slaying dragons?'

'Most of the dragons were sleazy criminals or wild-eyed fanatics, and many of the maidens not much better,' he said ironically. 'It was a sordid business at best, and although my father wouldn't have dreamed of asking me to give it up he certainly didn't approve.' His mouth twisted. 'The regular army was fine; covert operations were unprincipled and shady. Better be a soldier and die honestly than a spy and end up too crooked to know whether you had any principles left. He wasn't far wrong, either.'

'What made you do it?'

A coldly amused light glimmered in the depths of his eyes. 'Ideals, mainly. I thought I could make some sort of difference to the world, redress a balance that seemed to be tilting in the direction of evil. I was young and I thought I could make a difference.'

'You did make a difference. You saved my life,' she said. 'I haven't thanked you for that. It may not be worth much in the global view of things, but it's important to me.'

'It became important to me too.' He smiled at her startled glance. 'So important that after you were safe I decided I'd see how you were getting on when you were twenty-one and all grown up.'

It was like a thunderclap. Her eyes flew to his face, met a shimmering, enigmatic gaze. Well, two could play at this game, dangerous though it might be.

'What stopped you?' she asked, head high, her smile aching on her mouth.

'Common sense.' He spoke caustically, not sparing himself. 'I soon realised that although I thought I knew you well I'd been fooling myself. There is a basic and unalterable difference between the life I lead and yours.'

The pulse beat fast in her throat, but she managed to control her voice enough to say calmly, 'Poor little rich girl?'

'Exactly. I saw a photograph of you on the cover of *Tatler*, dressed in fifty million dollars' worth of blue diamonds. They were the same colour as your eyes, and you wore them with complete negligence, as though they were costume jewellery. Any ideas I might have had about meeting you again were just cobwebs tacked together by wishful thinking. So I did what any sensible man does. I cut down the cobwebs and got on with real life.'

She remembered that photograph. She hadn't wanted to do it, but it had been a sort of celebration after months in therapy working through fear and bitterness and rage as well as the ever-present pain of betrayal. Posing for the photographer had been a defiant gesture to fate and everything that conspired against her.

At that time it had seemed that the men who had kidnapped her would never be brought to justice. It was an enormous relief to learn that thanks to Adam and men like him—unnamed soldiers who fought their dirty war in the dark shadows at the edge of humanity—justice of some sort had been done.

'Don't tell me you waited with palpitating eagerness for me to come back,' he said harshly. 'I'll bet you did your best to forget.'

'I very carefully avoided thinking about it,' she agreed. Except for him. She had never been free of him. 'Tell me what being an agent was like.'

'So you've decided to believe me?'

'I got someone to check,' she said.

His smile was a nice blend of cynicism and assessment. 'Of course. And what did they find out?'

She told him. A frown gathered between his black brows. 'You've got good sources,' he said slowly.

'Yes. It won't go any further, Adam.'

Broad shoulders moved in a slight shrug. 'It doesn't really matter. It's over now. Most of it was dirty, far from romantic, and secret. You tell me about your life.'

Although his voice was neutral she discerned the faint note of scorn beneath the words, and felt like hitting him across his autocratic face. 'What would you like to know?' she asked sweetly.

His smile was cruel. 'How about your lovers?' he suggested with ice-cold malice. 'Tell me about the man you were engaged to. What happened?'

'That is none of your business.' The memory of her engagement still had the power to hurt her, especially when she was confronted by the cause of the whole fiasco.

'Didn't he measure up to your brother?'

'I don't know any man who measures up to Saul.'

He looked across the room to their waiter who immediately, as though that swift glance had been a summons, came over. 'We're ready,' Adam said.

When the food and wine had been ordered, and the little ceremony of the tasting gone through, the waiter poured them each a glass of excellent New Zealand Sauvignon Blanc and disappeared.

Adam looked at her. 'It doesn't augur well for your prospects if you can't find a man who measures up to Saul, does it?'

'I don't want to marry my brother,' she said, and sipped the cool, flowery liquid with gratitude. 'Or even a man like him.'

'Sensible woman.' A couple passed by, both smiling at Adam—the woman, Stephanie noted sourly, with definite coquetry.

'Friends of yours?' she asked, her eyes on the consciously seductive sway of slim hips in pleated chiffon as the woman undulated away from them.

'Acquaintances,' he said dismissively.

So the elegant, provocative invitation was wasted. Stephanie looked down at her hands, furious at the pang of jealousy that was only now subsiding. 'I believe New Zealand is in the throes of an election,' she said. 'What are the issues?'

Accepting the change of subject with a mocking glance, he told her what the issues were, concisely and, as far as she could judge, fairly. Over the years Stephanie had developed an interest in politics, so she was able to keep her end up. That subject lasted until the first course arrived, delicious Bluff oysters for him, kingfish in a subtly flavoured orange sauce for her.

'Now,' he said, after the waiter had poured more wine, 'what other neutral subject can we talk about?'

'The roses,' she suggested. 'I imagine you don't just breed on a whim, that you have some sort of plan. What exactly are you trying to do?'

'I'm trying to produce a good healthy bush which will grow and flower well in our humid, warm, temperate climate, with scent and form and a strong constitution,' he said evenly.

'So how do you go about doing that?'

He was fascinating, and obviously enjoyed his work, but Stephanie couldn't help wondering whether it filled his life. And if it didn't, what did? It was difficult to imagine a man who had walked on the edge for years settling down to breed roses with no hankering for the adrenalin and danger that had once been his constant companions.

'And do you miss your other career?' she asked a little daringly.

'Not in the least.' He scanned her face. 'Have I gone down in your estimation?' he asked. 'Does the prospect of danger excite you, Stephanie?'

She looked directly at him. 'Far from it,' she said, 'but it's been my experience, limited though it is, that people who are attracted to jobs where danger is a constant companion need that fix.'

'Those people,' he said implacably, 'die. And they take others with them. Adrenalin junkies don't last long—they forget that ninety per cent of any successful job is the preparation. No, I don't miss the excitement or the prospect of being stabbed in the back.' In his voice there was a sardonic weariness that she understood rather than heard.

'Who tried to kill you with a sword?' she asked abruptly.

'A Colombian drug baron. He was one of the customers for the nuclear weapons from Russia. He thought that as he was descended from Spanish *conquistadore* a sword was a more polished, not to say refined way of dispatching a nuisance than the guns and explosives his hired killers used.'

The muscles in her stomach clenched. 'What happened?'

'Fortunately I took fencing at school,' he said, and she knew that that was all she was going to hear.

An innocuous remark hovered on the tip of her tongue, but he forestalled it. 'What are you planning to do? Or do you have no plans?'

She looked at him coolly. 'I've taken over responsibility for my affairs,' she said.

'What affairs?'

Beneath the autumn-coloured silk her shoulders moved a fraction. 'Oh, there's a family trust, and stuff like that,' she said vaguely. 'At the moment I'm finding my way through the ramifications; then I'll see how I go as a manager.'

'It sounds a good life,' he said. 'You'll be able to attend charity balls to take your mind off the boredom of business matters.'

'I don't like them much,' she said. 'I intend to help with the real work of several charities.'

'Thereby salving your conscience?' he asked.

She smiled deliberately at him, letting her eyes wander down his angular face to linger on the straight, hard mouth with its surprisingly sensual bottom lip. 'Surely you're not going to allow me a conscience?' she said lightly. 'After all, I'm a spoilt rich kid, remember?'

He took the gibe with a slight backward jerk of his head that threw the slashing line of his jaw and chin into prominence. 'Am I being unbearable?' he asked, his voice dark and mocking, underpinning the words with a subtle intimacy that sent a swift prickle through her skin.

'No more so than you ever were,' she retorted.

He was watching her with hooded eyes, his face not softened by the smile that curved his mouth. Deep in the pit of her stomach a quick, involuntary shiver of awareness, that primal, intense response that only Adam seemed to evoke, stirred into life; she felt it progress to the base of her spine, and then diffuse through her, potent as old brandy.

She asked abruptly, 'Where did you go after you got out of Switzerland?'

'I can't tell you.' No emotion in his voice, not then, and not when he added, 'There's a lot of my life I can't talk about.'

'I see,' she said, picking up her fork.

'Did you consult a counsellor?'

She nodded. 'She was very good, and it did help. I had nightmares for a few months——' there was no need for him to know that she still got them occasionally '—but apart from that I've been fine.'

'The resilience of youth.'

His gently teasing voice surprised her into a smile. For a moment they were caught in a small bubble of awareness, eyes locked together as the restaurant and the other diners faded into a dimness. Then he made a comment about the food, and the bubble was broken.

They ate the rest of their meal with outwardly easy conversation, discussing books, a film made in New Zealand that had won several prestigious awards, the reason that modern roses were so prone to disease—it came in with genes from the yellow Persian rose—and whether tourism was going to be the salvation of the Pacific basin, and, if so, how it should be organised.

Adam made her think; he looked at things from a different angle, a slightly mordant, more practical point of view, and behind everything he said was a penetrating intelligence that had her reaching further than she ever had before.

Talking to him was exhilarating, like being on a roller-coaster with no fixed destination, and when eventually they'd drunk their coffee and it was time to go she saw with a feeling of astonishment that they were almost the last people in the restaurant.

In the car back to the hotel she said, 'That was a super evening, thank you very much.'

'You sound like a little girl,' he said. 'A very English little girl.'

'You sound English too. How is that?'

'My father met my mother in England and stayed on. Although we moved out to New Zealand when I was five they sent me back to school when I was eleven, so I never really lost the accent.'

'I see.' She looked across at the arrogant profile harshly outlined against the lights of the street outside, and said, 'I'll bet you got teased when you moved out to New Zealand.'

'Not after the first time,' he said. 'I was a young tough.'

Yes, she could imagine that. Would he have sons who were as tough as he'd been? She tried to resist, but an image of a much younger Adam slid into her brain, and she felt her heart clutch, deliquesce . . .

'Did you go to university?' she asked brightly to banish it.

His mouth tilted. 'No, straight into the army. I was determined to prove that having a rose-breeder for a father didn't weaken my masculinity.'

Surely—no, he had to be joking. She said solemnly, 'It must have been a great cross for you to bear.'

His mouth curved further but he said with equal seriousness, 'By the time I'd fought my way through the lower forms people were getting tired of calling me petal and blossom.'

That surprised her into a gurgle of laughter. 'Really?'

'They didn't try it after the first time. I was handy with my fists. And my size helped. I was always a lump of a boy.'

'I doubt whether you were ever lumpish in your life,' she said. Big, certainly, but it was impossible to imagine him moving with anything other than the easy masculine grace that was so much a part of his immediate impact.

'I was always six or seven inches taller than any other boy in the class.'

'It's all right for a boy,' she said, and immediately wished she hadn't.

'Were you teased?'

She nodded. 'Girls aren't allowed to clobber each other, and I wasn't quick-witted enough to defend myself with my tongue. Still, I got over it. By the time I was fifteen I was rather glad I towered over everyone.'

The car turned into the hotel forecourt. The door was opened with a flourish. Stephanie got out and Adam came around and took her elbow, his long, lean fingers resting lightly but with determination against silk warmed by her skin. She thought that tomorrow she'd have five little dots burned into her flesh.

'You don't need——' she began.

'I'll see you in,' he said calmly.

They were almost at the desk when someone said from behind, 'Miss Jerrard?'

Stephanie stiffened but didn't turn. She felt Adam's shockingly swift movement as he positioned himself between her and the intruder.

'Miss Jerrard,' the voice repeated, turning itself into Brett's distinctive tone.

'What do you want?' Adam's voice was deep and cold and forbidding as he turned to survey the interloper.

'I've got a message for Miss Jerrard.'

Stephanie said, 'What is it, Brett?'

'Your brother wants you to ring him immediately. He said it's important.'

'Thank you,' Stephanie said tonelessly, holding out her hand for the key. Candace, she thought, and without looking at either man set rapidly off towards the bank of lifts, her heels clicking on the marble floor. But when she reached the lift she stared at it for a moment, trying to remember what floor she was on.

A long arm reached out and stabbed the button. 'I'll come up with you,' Adam said without emphasis.

'Mr Jerrard wanted me to stay with her.' Brett wasn't objecting to Adam's presence, merely making it clear that he didn't intend to go.

In spite of the pressure in her chest Stephanie understood the younger man's attitude; Adam was not a man you tried to block.

Up in her room she put the call through to Fala'isi and stood with her head turned away, knuckles white as she gripped the receiver. Asa, their housekeeper answered.

'I'm sorry,' she said, 'but he's not here, Stephanie. Your sister isn't well, so he took her to the hospital. He's just rung to say that she's all right, but they're keeping her in tonight and he'll stay there. He'll ring you first thing tomorrow morning.'

Stephanie leaned against the wall, relief washing over her in great waves. 'She's not likely to lose the baby, is she?'

'It doesn't sound like it, so don't you go worrying about her, now. She's all right, and the baby is fine. I think she just got a bit hot, that's all. We've had a heat wave here for the last two days, and it's been raining all the time.'

'All right, I'll expect to hear from Saul in the morning. I'm coming home tomorrow anyway. Goodnight, Asa.'

She put the receiver down and turned to the two men, but it was Brett she addressed. 'Everything's all right,' she said. 'My sister's suffering a bit from heat exhaustion and had to go to hospital, but she's fine.'

'I'm glad to hear that,' he said, then looked at Adam, tall and somewhat possessive beside her.

Adam's smile had something tigerish and challenging about it. 'I'll stay for a while,' he said.

The other man's face was a study in indecision. He looked swiftly at Stephanie. 'Is that——'

'I'll take care of her,' Adam said smoothly, and to Stephanie's astonishment Brett's obvious worry began to dissipate, overwhelmed by the calm authority of the man beside her.

'All right,' he said, yielding to Adam's stronger will. 'Stephanie, I'll book you seats on the first Air New Zealand plane up in the morning.'

'Thank you very much. I'm sorry you had to break up your evening . . .'

'No problem,' he said. 'Well, goodnight, then.'

She saw him to the door, then turned, saying indignantly, 'What on earth did you think you were doing? You embarrassed the poor man——'

Adam put out a hand and drew her close against him, holding her, refusing to let her go. 'I've waited five long years for this,' he said quietly, and bent his head and kissed her.

'I wanted to do this the first time I saw you,' he said an aeon later, and kissed her again. 'You were terrified yet so valiant, with your thin wrists rubbed raw where you'd tried to free yourself.'

His mouth hovered over hers, so that she felt each word as well as heard it. 'And when you set your jaw and staggered up the mountainside with me, refusing to give in, then I knew I was in deep, deep trouble.'

'How could you?' she whispered, enchanted, yet unable to give up her suspicions so easily. 'You didn't show any signs—you slept beside me each night and never touched me once——'

His arms contracted tightly around her. 'I didn't do much sleeping, believe me,' he said grimly, 'and I was only able to keep to my side of the bed by reminding myself that you'd had a hell of a time, and only a sadist would force any sort of advance on to you.'

'You were very scathing that first morning when I—when we——'

'When I woke up and found you sprawled out over me in innocent abandon.' He laughed beneath his breath and tilted her chin so that he could see into her eyes.

His own were not soft—they could never be soft, she thought confusedly—but they gleamed with a certain rueful amusement, more gentle than ironic. 'You were utterly scathing!'

'I had to be cruel, otherwise I'd have taken you then and there, and God knows, I knew you weren't ready for it.'

'You told me I was a tart!'

'I wanted to frighten and offend you. I was getting far too interested in a girl I had to keep at a distance.'

'You needn't have been so brutal.'

'It was a measure of how much you affected me. You put me through hell,' he said roughly. 'Those long legs beneath my shirts, the way you snuggled up to me each night, the innocent open awareness I could see blossoming in you—I've never had such a difficult damned assignment. But I had to keep my hands off you because there was no room in my life for you then. I had a job to do.'

Although it was not particularly flattering to be second to a mission, she respected him for his determination and resolution. And now, with that equivocal, sensuous undertone roughened and lazy in her ears, she understood so much more than she had before.

'And do you have a job to do now?' she asked demurely.

'No,' he said, and his mouth came down on hers, and this time there was nothing tender about his kiss; he stamped possession on her, took his fill of her eager mouth, and she faced his strength and demand and met it and matched it.

It had been coming ever since he'd lifted her out of the makeshift coffin. The arid years of waiting and separation had served to whet the edge of the need and the hunger, making the traditional preliminaries unnecessary.

Stephanie didn't try to stop him when his fingers undid the silk at her breast. Indeed, she was busy freeing the studs on his shirt, her body aching with desire, her mind clouded by passion too long frustrated. Nevertheless, when his fingers touched her skin she shuddered, reacting with a swift abandon.

For a moment his big body clenched. He said hoarsely, 'You scare me.'

'Why?'

'I want you so much I'm afraid I'll hurt you.'

'You couldn't hurt me,' she said, because a great and glorious certainty wrapped her in its embrace. At long last it was, she thought, gazing into his narrowed, glittering eyes, the right time, the right place... Only to wonder almost immediately whether her confidence had been a little premature. She had never seen him naked, his body in the pride of his masculinity.

'We'll fit together perfectly,' he said, touching the full curves of her breasts with knowing fingers, seeming to relish the contrast between the pale, soft mounds and his lean hand, ivory skin and olive, light and dark, female and male in potent, age-old polarisation.

Her head fell back over his arm as he lowered his mouth and took the proud nipple into his mouth. Stephanie lay voluptuously exposed, her hands on the broad expanse of his chest, feeling the speeding thunder of his heart beneath her palms, the rhythm of his life.

Sensation ran like jagged arrows of ecstasy, like electric impulses connecting nerves and heart, joining skin and the deepening heat at the pit of her stomach, tightening every sinew and cell. Only once before had she experienced such delicious tension; she stretched, racked by delight, a conspirator in her own torment.

He was like a god, she thought, lifting heavy eyelids so that she could see him, glory in the steel muscles, the sleek, damp skin that caught across the sensitised tips of her questing fingers. As he made himself master of her responses, found his pleasure in the lush abundance of her body, she conquered the shyness that had been so long a part of her and fed her own desire with judicious exploration of all that made him a man.

He kissed her voraciously, hungrily, yet tempering his strength so that, although his hands trembled with the force of his passion and his mouth was hard and hot and almost angry, he didn't hurt her.

She was just as fierce, freeing the shackles of repressed longing, holding nothing back. She didn't fool herself that this was love; there had been nothing of love in his face, in his hands, in the predator's drive of his body.

'Adam,' she said thickly. 'Adam, please...'

'What do you want?'

'You. I want you.'

He laughed, the guttural, triumphant laugh of a lover, and kissed the shallow dimple of her navel. 'How?' he asked. 'How do you want me? Have you dreamed about this, princess, and woken shaking and starving and empty, untold times, until the craving became part of you, insatiable, gnawing at the roots of your heart? Is that how it is with you?'

A shiver gathered deep inside her, began to move through cells and nerves in ever-widening circles.

'Yes,' she whispered, 'that's exactly how it is.'

His hand moved down, down, found the slick centre of her heat, and she convulsed, crying out as her body bucked in his hands. Waves of sensation gripped her inexorably, tossed her higher and higher, beyond thought and reaction, so helplessly was she flung beyond anything she had ever experienced before.

And then it faded, and she clutched him.

'What's the matter?' he asked.

'You haven't—you didn't . . .'

His laugh was closer to a growl. 'No, not yet, my lovely.'

In the time that followed she learned of the myriad ways that a man could pleasure a woman; she learned that Adam could keep his self-control almost indefinitely, until eventually she grabbed him by the shoulders and demanded that he give her what she most wanted, reinforcing her command with a swift, forceful movement against the coiled strength of his loins that brought another of those soft laughs from him.

But the last laugh was on her. Fearlessly she looked up at a face drained of everything but the need to curb his desire; lips drawn back, the warm lamplight honing the planes and angles of his face into a mask of almost demonic intensity, he was exultant, primal man.

One powerful thrust took him home, stretched her so far that at first she thought she'd cry out with pain. Yet almost immediately the pressure eased. Eyes locked on the crystalline fire of his, she gasped. She saw comprehension and anger flare deep in the colourless depths, but when she pushed experimentally both emotions were replaced by the flickering of a heat that seared her.

It was a journey unlike any other. Almost instantly they set up a rhythm of giving and taking so intermingled that there was no difference, until at last, weakened by pleasure, she sobbed something, and was hurled back into that place where time ended and only sensation existed in its purest, almost unbearable form.

This time it was even better; his beloved weight added an unknown quality to the experience, and as she lay imprisoned by the fiery sweetness he joined her, his body arching in raw compulsion, his head thrown back as he too reached that place.

How sad, she thought as she lay beneath him, sweat-streaked bodies still joined, that there would be no child. He had made sure of that.

His chest fell and rose, until he turned on to his side and gathered her against him. In a deep, sensual, slow voice he asked, 'Why didn't you tell me it was the first time for you?'

A yawn cracked Stephanie's face. 'Does it matter?' she mumbled, trying to fight off waves of exhaustion.

'No.' He kissed her forehead. 'We'll talk about it in the morning. Go to sleep now.'

CHAPTER EIGHT

SOMETHING was buzzing in her ear, some lost bee, dive-bombing——

'Stephanie! Wake up, princess, someone's calling you on the phone. Stephanie! Come on, wake up and answer the bloody thing before I do!'

Duke's voice. No, Adam. Not Duke.

Slowly, with enormous reluctance, she reached out a hand and groped for the telephone, wondering at the feeling of boneless contentment that flooded her. 'Hello?' she muttered.

'I'm sorry to wake you, Stephanie, but it's Asa here, and I think you should get back here as soon as you can.'

'Asa?' Then she remembered. 'Asa, what's happened?'

'It's your sister. She's not well. Saul rang me ten minutes ago from the hospital and said you were to come back.'

'Has she lost the baby?'

'I don't know.'

Asa the unflappable, Asa whose serene Polynesian presence had always represented calmness and dignity, was crying. Stephanie sat bolt upright in the bed, clutching the receiver. The light flicked on.

She stared at Adam's unshaven countenance with blind appeal. 'What about Candace?' There was a short silence. Stephanie's heart contracted tightly in her chest. 'For God's sake, Asa, how is Candace?'

At last Asa said, 'She's not good, Stephanie.'

'Oh, God,' she whispered.

The receiver was taken from her hand. As he slid his other arm around her shoulders and held her close Adam

164

said crisply, 'I'm a friend of Stephanie's. Tell me exactly what is going on.'

It didn't seem strange to lean against his reassuring strength. Frantically trying to empty her mind of everything but calmness, Stephanie waited until he had finished listening, then asked abruptly, 'Where's Saul's Learjet?'

Something moved in his eyes, but he relayed the question. 'On it's way to China,' he said. 'No, it's all right. I'll get her up as soon as possible, probably within four hours.' He hung up.

'How?' Stephanie croaked.

He was already dialling another number. 'I know a man who runs a charter service out of Auckland,' he said. His warm hand held hers. 'His Learjet will take you there in less than three hours from take-off. I'll get him to land at Whenuapai—that's the Air Force field ten minutes from my nursery.'

'Can he do that?'

'I'll ask the commander as a favour.'

She said huskily, 'It's very kind of you, but I can't impose——'

'Don't be an idiot. Ring the maid and get her to pack.'

Shivering, she said, 'I'll pack. It will give me something to do. Oh, here, you'd better give him my credit-card number.'

He didn't look at the card she hauled out of her purse, so she put it down beside the telephone. Five minutes later when she came out of the bathroom it was still in the same place. As she pulled on jeans and T-shirt, then began to stuff the rest of her clothes and toiletries into her bag, she heard his voice, calm and cool and confident. He didn't sound as though he was asking a favour. It was difficult, she thought wearily, to imagine Adam asking favours of anyone.

A couple of minutes later he put the receiver down and said, 'It will be ready when we are. I'll pick up some clothes and a passport on the way.'

She said, 'I can't let you come with me.'

'Don't be an idiot,' he said. He got up, as beautiful and powerful, as potently evocative as a bronzed statue of some antique time when only the most perfect athletes were chosen to represent gods, and began to dress.

She should protest, but the thought of three hours by herself in the Learjet, sick with fear, kept her silent. Sitting down, she pulled on a pair of shoes. 'I'll ring Brett,' she said.

On the way out along the motorway she muttered, 'I'm afraid, Adam.'

He glanced her way. 'It's almost certain to be a false alarm. Doting husbands are notoriously easily upset.'

'Not Saul.'

'In that case you'll have to face whatever happens. But people rarely die out of the blue like that, Stephanie.'

'I know,' she whispered. 'But there are always exceptions.'

His hand dropped over her restless ones, squeezed hard, and resumed its place on the wheel. He didn't say anything, but his silent understanding eased a little of her fear and foreboding.

Dawn saw them a hundred miles out from Fala'isi, flying over a sea that began as the colour of a dove's breast, the purest, softest grey, then changed, as the glowing hues of the sunrise faded in the east, to a brilliant, saturated emerald. Ahead on the horizon was the cloud that clung to the island's mountainous core, the cloud that had drawn the ancient Polynesian navigators across the endless expanse of the Pacific. Usually Stephanie's heart lifted when she saw it white in the sapphire sky; this morning she felt only dread.

'All right?'

Adam's voice in her ears dragged her from her thoughts. She nodded and gave him a bleak smile. 'Yes, thank you.'

The Learjet arrowed north with all the verve and speed of a humming-bird. Since they'd left the Air Force base Adam had insisted she talk to him; whenever she had fallen into frightened silence he had revived the conversation, his confident voice helping to ward off the dreadful images of Candace ill and dying.

She had learned that it took seven years from breeding a rose to marketing it, so none of the roses coming out under his name was yet of his breeding. However, he had several coming on with which he planned to win both the All-American Award and the European Championship.

'My father won that, the Golden Rose of the Hague, twice,' he'd said.

Stephanie had looked at him. 'So you plan to win three times?'

'I believe in building on what's already been done. We have a good name, and it's going to be even more highly regarded by the time I die.'

She'd said, 'How do you choose roses to breed from?'

'It's all a matter of eye.'

'Candace said it would be genetics.' Her mouth had tightened suddenly. 'She said you'd have to be ruthless.'

'Why?'

'Oh, because you must plant so many seeds, then cull most of them.'

'I suppose ruthlessness comes into it.' He'd sounded amused. 'Out of fifty thousand or so seedlings I might end up with twenty roses, and out of those I might choose only one to patent.'

'I didn't know you could patent plants.'

'New Zealand has plant breeders' rights that last for twenty years. Until they were legislated for plant-breeding was a hobby; nobody could actually earn a living from it.'

Desperate to keep her mind off what was waiting for them, she had asked, 'How do you prove that your rose is a good one?' and listened while he told her of the budding sticks sent overseas to rose trial grounds where they were grown and evaluated, of the tightly inter-woven old boys' network that was the world of roses, of triumphs and failures, of the different ambitions rose-breeders had for their seedlings. Some wanted elegantly stemmed beauties for cutting, some bred for long-flowering bushes for the garden, some searched obsess-ively for rare and unusual shades of colour.

She said now, with a twisted smile. 'Thank you.'

'Why?'

'For—oh, for being kind. You always seem to be res-cuing me.'

'Hardly.' His voice was dry, as though she had hit a nerve. 'This doesn't constitute a rescue. A helping hand, possibly.'

'Are you sure there isn't anyone who's going to miss you?'

'If you mean someone with claims on me, then no,' he said bluntly. 'Don't worry, princess.'

'I used to hate it when you called me that.'

His smile was mocking. 'I didn't intend you to like it.'

'So why did you do it?'

'To remind myself of the distance between us. And the lies.'

The pilot's voice came through the speakers. 'OK, strap yourselves in; we're landing in ten minutes.'

Although there was nobody there to meet them, it was obvious that everyone on the island knew why Stephanie had come back. They were waved through Customs with a speed and efficiency tempered by warm, unspoken sympathy that had her groping futilely for her handkerchief.

'Here,' Adam said from beside her, and thrust an im-maculate one into her hand.

She was glad of his presence. To her he was invin-cible, so that nothing bad could happen if he was beside her. Stupid, and wrong, clutching at straws, but it was a small comfort, one she clung to, because no one had told her that Candace was better. Knowing how swiftly news ran through the island community, she understood that this must mean her sister was still in danger. Anguish and dread twisted her heart.

Outside she blinked in the brilliant sunlight, temporarily stunned by its heat and the humidity.

'Is that your car?' Adam said calmly, indicating a large, dusty vehicle just drawing up beneath a magnificent raintree.

'Yes.'

He nodded and set off towards it. Obediently Stephanie followed him, recognising the man who was coming towards them, his handsome brown face set in lines of gravity and concern. It was Apiolu, who acted as chauffeur for Saul in between fishing forays.

'Morning, Stephanie,' he said, grabbing the bags from the porter.

She introduced the two men, then asked urgently, 'How is she?'

The islander's pleasant, blunt features tightened. 'Not too good,' he said briefly. 'Saul wants you at the hospital straight away.'

Colour drained from her face. She put out a shaking hand, which was caught by Adam as he hustled her inside the car, saying curtly, 'Take deep breaths, in through your nose, and exhale through your mouth. Fainting isn't going to help you or your brother or sister.'

He was an unfeeling bastard, but she did as he said, and the icy nausea faded, to be replaced by something perilously close to terror. She said aloud, as she had been saying silently ever since the call, 'Women don't die in childbirth any longer, not in the western world. Candace is strong. And the hospital is an excellent one. Grant endowed it.'

'Who's Grant?'

'A cousin. A distant cousin. Grant Chapman. He's the paramount chief of the island.'

'How did that happen?'

He persuaded her to talk about her family's connection to the island, about the original buccaneering Chapman who had landed on the island at a time when most of its inhabitants had been killed by assorted exploiters and the diseases they brought, and who, to his shock, had been recognised as the saviour promised by prophecy. Forced to marry the paramount chief's only child, he had reluctantly grown into the role assigned to him, and the direct descendant of that union, Grant Chapman, was now paramount chief in his turn.

'I didn't realise a chiefdom could pass through the female line,' Adam said.

Stephanie knew what he was doing, but she was grateful nevertheless. While she was telling him about these colourful ancestors she wasn't worrying quite so futilely about Candace.

'She had immense prestige and power,' she told him. 'It was understood from her birth that she would do great things. And the Polynesians are a pragmatic people. Family is of vital importance, more so than the individual. If the chief's son wasn't strong enough to hold the tribe together, someone else of the same lineage who did have the necessary qualities would be chosen.'

'What about the original Chapman?'

'He gained authority from his ruthlessness when it came to fighting off the assorted blackbirders and pearl pirates and sandalwood-cutters, and the marriage gave him the necessary tribal *mana*, especially when his wife produced three sons.'

'He sounds fairly intimidating.'

'I think they both were. For the last five years I've thought he probably bore a startling resemblance to you.' She looked at him, and said with a quivering smile, 'Some of the stories about his wife would make your hair curl. Their marriage wasn't a romantic South Sea idyll; it was quite literally a fight for life.'

The car drew up outside the hospital. Stephanie's voice wavered; she swallowed, and for a moment her hand was covered and held in a solid, comforting grip.

'Is your sister a fighter?' Adam asked.

She lifted wet eyes to his. 'Oh, yes.'

'That's the most important thing,' he said. 'Because they were fighters I've seen people recover from wounds that should have killed them several times over.'

They were met at the door by a deputation comprising the matron and the medical superintendant. In a voice that barely trembled, Stephanie asked, 'How is she?'

Candace had, it appeared, been gravely ill, but was now on the mend.

Clinging to Adam's hand, Stephanie looked from one grave face to the other and said, 'Can I see her?'

The medical superintendant traded a glance with the matron. 'She wants to see you, but she's still very sick. Can you just let her know that you're here, and then come away?'

'Yes, of course.'

Adam's grip was warm and strong. Stephanie introduced him as they all went across the highly polished floor and into the lift; the hospital was built of wood on a hill overlooking the town and the sea, and, although only two storeys high, was as modern and up-to-date as any in the Pacific.

Candace was in the small critical care unit; the matron took Stephanie in. As she opened the door she leaned closer and murmured, 'She's going to be all right.'

But fear chilled Stephanie's swift relief as she took in the still, unresponsive figure in the bed, and the tall form of her brother, his arrogant face lean and haggard, holding his wife's hand as he bent over her and spoke, low, insistent words meant only for her ears.

Saul looked up. Accurately judging her emotions, he said softly, 'She's going to make it, Steph.'

'Oh, thank God,' Stephanie breathed, taking her sister's other hand in hers. 'I thought I might get here too late...'

'For few minutes I thought that too.' Saul touched his wife's cheek. Unconscious though she was, a smile curved her mouth. As though he couldn't help himself, he bent his head and kissed her.

Stephanie asked, 'What was the matter?'

'Toxaemia. It can happen in pregnancy, and apparently her doctor in London told her to watch for it. She didn't want to upset me, so she didn't say anything, but she gave Losa Penia her medical notes, and as she's been going to him each week he knew exactly what it was and how to deal with it.'

'And it's not going to come back?'

'It doesn't go away. She'll have to stay under observation until the baby's born.'

'Another month. Is the baby all right?'

'Yes, thank God. And I won't be going away from now on. Candace is far more important to me than anything else in my life, infinitely more important than Jerrard's.'

'I know,' Stephanie said serenely. 'So does she.'

'I hope so.' He lifted his eyes from his wife's calm, pale face. 'How did you get here so quickly?'

Stephanie made a small grimace. 'Hired a Learjet. We came up in that.'

'We?'

She said quietly, 'Nobody you know, although you know of him. He's Adam Cowdray. He also happens to be the man who rescued me from that crypt five years ago.'

Candace moaned something as Saul's fingers crushed hers. 'Sorry, my darling,' he said, holding them to his mouth. He kissed their pale limpness before turning to Stephanie and saying through thin lips, 'That man is a criminal.'

'As it happens, he isn't.' She held up her hand to stem the words she could see forming on his tongue. 'I'm not a complete idiot, Saul. I got London to run a check on him. Apparently he was working for some organisation in England, very hush-hush——'

'Stephanie, he's spun you a nice tale——'

'Saul, *listen* to me——'

'Stop it, you two, and let me be ill in some degree of peace,' Candace muttered drowsily.

Face transfigured, Saul slid to his knees by the side of the bed. 'Darling,' he said in a voice Stephanie had never heard before. 'Oh, God, darling, don't you ever do that to me——'

Stephanie got up and left them, her throat thick with unexpressed emotions, her eyes bright. She had no right to be there; it seemed voyeuristic to eavesdrop on her brother's nakedly innermost emotions.

Before she got out of the ward she despised herself for wondering whether any man would ever look at her like that, with his heart in his eyes, stripped of everything but his love. Not Adam, she thought, swallowing hard. Never Adam. In spite of the incandescence of their lovemaking he hadn't said anything about loving her, anything at all except that she was beautiful, that he had wanted her for so long...

He had delivered the heaven he'd promised her, but love didn't enter into the equation at all.

'Stephanie?' He touched her arm.

She stared up into eyes that held all the world in their watchful, blue-white depths, and said, 'She's going to be all right. She told us to stop fighting and let her be ill in peace.' Her voice trembled and tears ached behind her lashes.

His hands caught her arms, held her upright with a bruising grip. 'You need something to eat and a cup of good strong coffee—and I don't care whether you still don't like it, that's what you're going to have. Sit down and I'll be back in five minutes.'

Somehow he procured a croissant, hot and buttery, a sliced papaw chilled to just the right degree with passion-fruit pulp lending its tang, and coffee whose fragrance lifted her heart immediately.

'Didn't you get any for yourself?' she asked.

He said dismissively, 'I'm not hungry. Eat up.'

She had eaten the food and was halfway through the cup of coffee when Saul emerged. 'How is she?' she asked urgently.

After one comprehensive glance at the man beside her Saul looked at her. No emotion gleamed in the blue eyes; nothing was revealed in his expression. 'She wants to see you,' he said.

Stephanie's gaze flicked from one strong-boned, implacable face to the other. Although Saul was tall and well-built, Adam was a couple of inches taller and his shoulders were wider, but both men took up the same amount of psychic space. Arrogant as lions, they snatched her breath away. Or they would have, if the antagonism neither was making any attempt to hide hadn't crackled so ominously about them.

'All right,' she said crossly. 'Play your stupid masculine games. But I warn you——'

'Stephanie,' Adam interrupted quite gently, 'go and see your sister.'

With what came very close to a flounce she walked away and left them there.

Candace lay with her eyes closed and her skin still too pale, but she opened them as Stephanie came in and said, 'What was the rose like?'

'Who cares about the wretched rose? How dare you do this and scare the hell out of everyone?'

Her half-sister grinned. 'Sorry, I'm sure! Saul just panicked. I'm going to be perfectly all right in a few days. I was worried about the baby, but Losa assures me it's fine, so all's well.'

Stephanie bent and kissed her, saying fiercely, 'Don't do it again! You terrified everyone. I've never seen Saul look like that, never.'

Candace's lashes drifted down. 'That's the problem with loving someone,' she said dreamily. 'It's those hostages to fortune. But there's no other way, really...'

Stephanie looked around wildly for the nurse, who came forward and soothed, 'She's just gone off to sleep. That's what she needs now, sleep and rest.'

'Thank you.' For a few moments Stephanie stood looking down at her sister's peaceful face before turning away.

She didn't know what she expected to see outside the ward. Blood on the floor, possibly; she certainly didn't think she'd see the two most important men in her life conducting what one glance told her was an outwardly reasonable conversation. Both men were experts in controlling their body language, so she couldn't work out how amicable their conversation was, but as she approached both looked up.

And suddenly she laughed, because both dark faces were stamped with an identical expression of watchful reserve. They were, she thought, two of a kind, the men in her life.

Saul fell silent and she could feel the tension sizzle out to meet her. The fans in the ceiling lazily swished air already heated by the rapidly rising sun, and everywhere was the smell of the tropics—frangipani and coconut oil, salt from the ever-present sea, and the tangy, elemental scent of fecundity.

'Have you had fun?' she asked, acid-sweet, looking from one non-committal set of features to the other.

'It's been interesting,' Saul said guardedly. 'Why don't you two go home? I'll stay here for the rest of the day, but there's no reason for you to.'

Stephanie looked at Adam, the man she loved with all her heart, and said steadily, 'Are you going back with the Learjet?'

'It's already gone.' His hard mouth relaxed fractionally. 'Your brother has asked me to stay on.'

She wouldn't look at Saul. She wouldn't! Keeping her eyes fixed on Adam's face, she said in her best social tone, 'Well, that's fine. Shall we go?'

He didn't like her cool relegation of him to guest status; a savage flare of emotion lit the crystalline depths of his eyes, was immediately controlled. Good, she thought angrily. He liked to play things really cool—two could do that. Perhaps he'd realise what it was like to be the one shut out.

So she persisted with her best hostess behaviour all the way to the house, pointing out the local sights, carefully avoiding Adam's eyes, and all the time his anger, disciplined yet as threatening as a bushfire flickering beyond distant hills, beat against her.

Asa was waiting. As Stephanie knew she would, she gave Adam a swift glance, lifted her brows, then showed him to the guest room next to Stephanie's.

'Where are you?' he asked as Stephanie prepared to go out.

'Next door,' she told him colourlessly.

This time it was his brows that shot up. 'A trusting soul, isn't she?' he asked, looking at the door Asa had left by.

Stephanie's mouth twitched. 'I think she'd just about given up on me,' she said cynically, and only her heart knew that she waited breathlessly for some sign, some indication, however tiny, that he cared more for her than just as a willing sexual partner.

He gave her a long, considering look. 'I don't intend to sleep with you in your brother's house,' he said.

Stephanie knew her smile was stiff and meaningless. 'How touchingly conventional,' she said.

His smile had no trace of humour in it; it was a warning and a promise at once, although he ignored the open provocation of her comment. 'But I am not here as your brother's guest,' he said quietly. 'I'm here because of you, and if you don't realise it yet perhaps this will help fix it in your mind.'

The kiss was almost brutal, as though he was staking a claim. Certainly the hands that slid the length of her body, moulding her against him with explicit promise, were not tender. He was aroused, as aroused as she was by the time his head lifted. Breathing hard, he said, 'You'd better get some sleep. You only had an hour or so last night.'

She didn't feel tired, but neither did she feel up to coping with Adam in his present mood. Refusing to acknowledge the heat that flamed across her skin or the passionate hunger summoned by his touch, she said, 'I'll do that. Asa will get you some breakfast if you want any, and then perhaps you should rest too.'

First, of course, she went to see the children. Safe with Peri—nursemaid, good friend and never-ending source of tales—they were curious but not alarmed by their parents' absence. Stephanie spent some time with them, at first explaining why Candace wouldn't be home that day, and then promising to take them to see their mother when the doctor said they could. Finally tiredness drove her to her bedroom.

She didn't expect to sleep, but she did, heavy eyelids almost immediately blocking her view of the huge timbers that supported the thatched roof of pandanus fronds. Saul's beach house was built in the same style as the fales of the island chiefs, and like them it was magnificently cool without the need for air-conditioning.

She woke to an evening perfumed with dusk, the brief, heart-stopping moment of hesitation between the open, brash beauty of the tropical day and the mystery and glamour of night. A look at the bedside clock had her sitting up, horrified, to ring the hospital.

Candace was fine, getting better by the minute, she was told.

Humming a little tune, she climbed from the bed and drifted towards her bathroom. By the time she had washed her hair, brushed it dry and wound herself in one of the cotton pareus she kept in her drawer, the all-purpose island outfit that looked so good with her long legs, the velvet Pacific night had completely enveloped the island. Absently aware of the gentle rustling of the palm fronds, she went out on to the terrace and walked swiftly past Adam's empty room, pausing at the smooth, twigless branches of a heavily scented frangipani to pick a cream and gold flower and tuck it behind her ear.

There had been no wind for weeks, so the ocean-circling waves that could sometimes smash down on the reef were barely audible. Wooed by the ravishing spell of the South Seas, she stood for a moment looking down over the thickly forested bank to the beach below, a proper Robinson Crusoe beach where the sand was white, coarsely crushed coral, and the coconut palms leaned on elegant grey stems towards the lagoon.

She loved Fala'isi, but the quickening in her body had nothing to do with her pleasure at being there. Adam waited for her, and during her sleep she had made the decision not to worry about the future. She would take everything he had to offer, and when the time came to say goodbye she would do that with grace and style, and then, perhaps, freed from this heated desire that had bedevilled her for years, she would be able to get on with her life.

She heard their voices before she saw them. They were sitting in chairs out on the terrace, and just before she saw the blur of their light shirts the clear, bell-like song of the tikau bird floated through the soft air. Of course she had heard it before—although a denizen of the high peaks, it occasionally came down to the coast—but a local legend said that if you heard the exquisite roulade in the company of the one you loved it meant that your love was reciprocated.

Although Stephanie didn't believe every old legend she'd been told, that didn't stop her heart from speeding

up at the sweet, seductive call. Perhaps, just this once,
it might be true?

Stopping, she looked through the scented darkness
towards the terrace where the men sat. She wanted to
see Adam, but not with Saul watching, not when she
had to be polite and fence with words against a background of tension that cut into her heart. Turning away,
she walked down the steep path to the beach.

She didn't hear him coming behind her; she didn't
know anyone was there until he put his hand on her
shoulder just as she reached the sand.

Stephanie reacted instantly. She lashed out, but he was
ready for the flat-handed blow, and before the lethal edge
could catch his throat he'd countered it. She was good,
but he was better, and within seconds she was held so
completely that she couldn't move.

'I'll bloody talk to whoever taught you to do that,'
he said through gritted teeth. 'One of these days you're
going to kill someone.'

'No. It's all right, I'm sorry,' she panted. 'You took
me by surprise, that's all. You can let me go now.'

'Put her down,' Saul said from just up the hill, a note
in the command that would have made any other man
drop her.

Instead Adam said curtly, 'Get out of here. This is
between Stephanie and me.'

'Stephanie?'

Adam said grimly, 'It's all right, I won't let her hurt
me. You're going to have to stop this habit she seems to
have developed of trying to kill anyone who comes up
behind her.'

'I did not try to kill you,' she said furiously, because
the conversation was slipping away from her. 'Damn
you, if I'd tried to kill you I'd have made a much better
fist of it. I've learnt a hell of a lot since I was kidnapped.'

Unbelievably, Saul laughed. 'She's right, you know.
You'd better be aware of what you're getting into.'

He was talking to them both, but mainly to Adam, who let her go, and asked interestedly, 'Has she learned to cook?'

'Why don't you ask her?' And to Stephanie's horror her brother turned away.

She opened her mouth to call him and Adam said quietly, 'Go with him now and you'll have made your choice forever.'

The moon had come out, huge and round and full, a lovers' moon, the moon the South Pacific had made her own, the moon of trade winds and spice breezes and the tikau bird. In its kindly light Adam looked cold and forbidding, the harsh features of his face set in obdurate granite.

He said quite calmly, the mask of control once more firmly in place, 'I'd have thought your teacher would have made sure you didn't go off half cocked like that.'

'You gave me a fright and I lashed out.' She hesitated, then said, 'Yes, well, he'd have my head if he saw what I did. I am sorry.'

She had never reacted with such lack of control before, and it was Adam who had tilted her off-balance, rubbed her nerves raw and stripped away her self-possession. Defensively, she attacked. 'You were angry before you touched me. Why?'

He looked at her for a moment, then turned so swiftly that she flinched and chopped his hand down on to the solid trunk of the closest coconut palm. It must have hurt, but he didn't flinch. 'Why are you pushing me away? You wanted me to go back on the Learjet, you spent the trip back from the hospital setting me at a distance, and you deliberately turned away when you saw me with Saul tonight.'

The first hectic charge of adrenalin was fading now and she was feeling exhausted and depressed, all energy drained from her. 'I'm not—I didn't——' She stopped, searching for words.

'It won't work,' he said harshly. 'I won't let you pull away, not now.'

A shimmering hope began to grow in her heart. She turned away and leaned back against the bole of the nearest palm, looking out over the lagoon. Moonlight had blocked out many of the stars and those that were left were robbed of much of their glory, but a silver snood cast on the surface of the sea gleamed like the pathway to glory, glittering across the sand, edging the fronds of the palms with silver.

Resolutely Stephanie kept her eyes on the silhouette of one of the tiny islands that the sea and the sand had thrown up on the edge of the barrier reef. Feeling her way, she said, 'I don't know what you want, Adam.'

'I want you.' He spoke slowly, in a flat, emotionless tone. He hesitated, before finishing, 'I would have told you this morning, only—it seemed crass, when you were so worried about your sister.'

'Told me what? That you want me? Last night rather proved that.'

Exasperated, he bit out, 'That I love you, of course.'

Equally shortly, she retorted, 'There's no *of course* about it!'

'Oh, for God's sake!' Before she had time to work out what he was doing he turned her and swept her into his arms. His mouth came down on hers in a kiss that burnt through the barriers she had set up, the painfully maintained defenses.

At last he lifted his mouth and said in a voice that had been stripped of everything but raw need, 'I *wanted* you right from the start. How I kept my hands off you I'll never know, but you were only eighteen, a virgin, sheltered and loved and protected, and I was seven cynical, hard years older, and I couldn't remember when there hadn't been women for the taking. I was doing a job that had to be done, a dangerous job where both our lives depended on my not putting a foot wrong. But whenever I looked at you I forgot about the job and wanted to get you out of there. Too much was at stake. I couldn't have done my job properly. I almost certainly put the whole scheme in danger because I wanted to protect you, not use you. And I had to use you. That was the beginning of the end for me.'

'The beginning of what end?'

Her eyes were snared by the splintered ice of his. His mouth tightened. 'That was when I realised I'd had enough of killing, of darkness and deceit and men with minds like calculators. You were the catalyst; I terrorised you and humiliated you, gave you traumas that might last a lifetime, lied to you——'

He laughed, and there was something straight from hell in the sound. 'That's what I was trained for, princess. To lie so well that no one would be able to catch me out in the truth. I'm very good at it. I've lied to men who were born lying, and got away with it.'

'Don't,' she said, understanding at last. 'Adam— don't.'

'I could promise that I'll never lie to you again,' he said in a level monotone, 'but that might be the biggest lie of all. I built a life on lies, Stephanie. I thought I could leave it behind me, but the past reaches its filthy hand out over the future, and I know now that I can't expect you to trust me. I've caused you enough grief, betrayed you in ways you don't even comprehend. When I sent you down the mountain into your brother's arms that night in Switzerland I had every intention of coming back for you; it wasn't until I came home to New Zealand and sanity that I realised what I'd done to you. And then I knew it was impossible.'

'You could have given me the choice,' she snapped.

'Oh, I knew I could have you,' he said coolly. 'But although making love to you is like finding paradise, I want more than that from you. I want your trust, and I know I can never have it. You showed that when you turned on me just now.'

He spoke calmly, without self-pity, with complete conviction.

Stephanie tried to sort out her emotions, and realised that he meant it; he wasn't going to persuade her, or try to coax her into either love or marriage. He honestly believed that he had put himself beyond the pale.

However, he wasn't going to let her go; that gave her hope.

She didn't dare look at him. This was something that had to be done without falling prey to the smouldering sexuality that flamed between them.

Her hands clenched by her sides. And then, quite suddenly, it was easy. All she really had to ask herself was whether she loved him, not the hero who had saved her from the crypt, not the man who caught every woman's eye, not the man whose potent male charisma wove a dark spell about her, but Duke, the man who had lived a life of lies and still wondered whether he was caught in their lingering webs.

'Of course I trust you,' she said.

'Just like that?'

She turned her face away from the silver glory, the perilous enchantment of the moon, and looked into the shuttered face of the man she loved. 'Yes, because I love you,' she said casually.

There was silence, and then he said dangerously, 'You little bitch,' and reached for her and caught her in his arms, holding her so close that she gasped. 'Are you a direct descendant of that island chieftainess and the buccaneer?' he asked.

'Yes.'

'I see.' His mouth hovered over hers. 'I can see I'm going to have my work cut out for me. Kiss me.'

Oddly shy, she looked into the blazing fire of his eyes. Then she reached up and pulled his head down and kissed him, her mouth demanding and eager, until he took over and they lost themselves in the world of passion and love reciprocated.

A long time later he lifted his head and surveyed her face with such complete male satisfaction that she laughed.

'We have to talk,' he said, leaning back against a convenient palm tree before taking her more gently in his arms and resting his cheek on her head. 'Don't wriggle. When you do that I can't concentrate.'

'What do we need to talk about now?'

'Your money,' he said, a note of irony hardening his voice.

'Oh, Adam, for heaven's sake, don't tell me you've got old-fashioned ideas about marrying money. Although actually the old-fashioned idea was that it was perfectly all right to marry money.'

'When both understood that after the necessary children were born it was fine to find love outside the marriage,' he said harshly. 'I'm not so damned accommodating, princess.'

'Neither am I,' she retorted smartly.

He gave her a small shake. 'Listen, will you?'

But he didn't speak immediately. Stephanie rested her head against his neck and smiled secretly at the rapid throbbing of his pulse.

He said reflectively, 'It's not so much the money, I suppose, it's the life.'

'Don't give me that rubbish about the difference in our situations.'

His smile was hard and narrow and mirthless. 'Because you're a modern woman and I'm a modern man? That's nonsense and you know it. You've grown up with money beyond most people's dreams—you're so accustomed to it that you don't even think of it—but if it was taken away you'd miss it.'

'You think I'm incredibly shallow,' she said, hiding her concern with delicate scorn.

'I think you're being deliberately obtuse,' he said sharply. 'Shallowness has nothing to do with it. Think, Stephanie.'

'It works very well for Saul and Candace,' she said stubbornly, hardly knowing what he was implying. Did he mean marriage?

'Nobody had to give up anything in that relationship.' His voice was impatient.

'You're a total chauvinist,' she retorted. 'Candace had to give up her anonymity, and believe me, she found that difficult. Anyway, where is all this talk of giving things up leading to?'

He put her to one side and looked out over the lagoon, his profile angled with a fierce beauty against the seductive silver and black nocturne of the night. He said evenly, 'I love you. I don't care what you do with your money, but if you marry me your life will be very different from the life you lead now. You've called me arrogant a couple of times, but you have your own brand of high-handedness, and the two of us are going to be dynamite together. It isn't going to be easy, princess.'

'Let's do a deal,' she said demurely. 'I'll stop calling you arrogant if you stop calling me princess.'

He laughed. 'No. That's how I think of you, as a princess.' His voice altered, the deep note of sensuality slowing his clipped intonation into a drawl. '*My* princess.'

She said, 'You can call me that for the rest of our lives, then.'

Much later that night Saul warned, 'Do you know what you're getting into? He's a hard man, and a possessive one.'

'I know. Adam's already told me that.' She added on an acerbic note, 'I'm not stupid, you know. I can see the pitfalls; what neither of you seem to realise is that life without him is flat and tasteless. I'd rather be shouting at him than living in perfect peace by myself.'

He laughed. 'I suppose you don't have that hair for nothing. Well, if you want it you have my blessing.'

'Do you like him?'

He shrugged. 'Would it matter if I didn't?'

'It would matter, but it's not going to make any difference.'

'As it happens, I do.'

He hadn't expected to, she knew, and in some ways it was surprising that they had got past the suspicion so quickly; they were too much alike to enjoy a simple camaraderie.

'Just as well,' she said peacefully. 'He likes you too.'

He laughed wryly. 'Well, he will when he realises that he has all of your heart.' He looked at his watch and got to his feet. 'I'd better be off; I'm going to sleep at the hospital. Candace made me come home so that I could deal with your Adam, and if I know her she's lying in her bed dying quietly of curiosity. You've got yourself quite a man there, little sister. But then, he's got enough woman to keep him busy for the rest of his life.'

About twenty minutes later Stephanie walked out of the wide door of her room, along the terrace and into the open door of the room next door.

'I said,' Adam's voice came through the darkness with a note of humour in it, 'that I wasn't going to make love to you under your brother's roof.'

She laughed and moved across the floor to the big bed. 'That's all right. I'd be the last person to try to make you change your mind. You just lie there and think of England while I make love to you.'

She slid beneath the sheet and leaned over him, kissing the straight line of his mouth. 'I love you,' she said softly.

As she had expected, he was naked. 'I can see that I'm going to have a hell of a time with you,' he said against her lips. 'Do you think that kissing you back is included in making love?'

'No, of course not.'

And in laughter and gentleness, in moments of sublime savagery and others of heart-shaking tenderness, they formed a pattern for their life together, a life without lies.

HARLEQUIN PRESENTS®

Harlequin brings you the best books, by the best authors!

Coming next month:

Harlequin Presents #1785
Last Stop Marriage by Emma Darcy

Award-winning author
"Pulls no punches..."—*Romantic Times*

Dan's wanderlust had spelled the end of his marriage to
Jayne...or *had* it?

But if he despised stability, how could he suddenly be a
daddy, and to *such* a cute baby?

Jayne found herself hoping that the last stop on Dan's
journey would be a passionate reunion...with her!

Harlequin Presents #1786
Dark Apollo by Sara Craven

"Ms. Craven does a magnificent job."—*Romantic Times*

Nik Xandreou *dared* to accuse Camilla's sister of being
a gold digger. So a furious Camilla set out to prove
Nik wrong! But in the clash of personalities that followed,
Camilla found herself hoping that Nik would win their
contest *and* her heart.

Harlequin Presents—the best has just gotten better!
Available in January wherever Harlequin books are sold.

TAUTH-4

MILLION DOLLAR SWEEPSTAKES (III)

No purchase necessary. To enter, follow the directions published. Method of entry may vary. For eligibility, entries must be received no later than March 31, 1996. No liability is assumed for printing errors, lost, late or misdirected entries. Odds of winning are determined by the number of eligible entries distributed and received. Prizewinners will be determined no later than June 30, 1996.

Sweepstakes open to residents of the U.S. (except Puerto Rico), Canada, Europe and Taiwan who are 18 years of age or older. All applicable laws and regulations apply. Sweepstakes offer void wherever prohibited by law. Values of all prizes are in U.S. currency. This sweepstakes is presented by Torstar Corp., its subsidiaries and affiliates, in conjunction with book, merchandise and/or product offerings. For a copy of the Official Rules send a self-addressed, stamped envelope (WA residents need not affix return postage) to: MILLION DOLLAR SWEEPSTAKES (III) Rules, P.O. Box 4573, Blair, NE 68009, USA.

EXTRA BONUS PRIZE DRAWING

No purchase necessary. The Extra Bonus Prize will be awarded in a random drawing to be conducted no later than 5/30/96 from among all entries received. To qualify, entries must be received by 3/31/96 and comply with published directions. Drawing open to residents of the U.S. (except Puerto Rico), Canada, Europe and Taiwan who are 18 years of age or older. All applicable laws and regulations apply; offer void wherever prohibited by law. Odds of winning are dependent upon number of eligible entries received. Prize is valued in U.S. currency. The offer is presented by Torstar Corp., its subsidiaries and affiliates in conjunction with book, merchandise and/or product offering. For a copy of the Official Rules governing this sweepstakes, send a self-addressed, stamped envelope (WA residents need not affix return postage) to: Extra Bonus Prize Drawing Rules, P.O. Box 4590, Blair, NE 68009, USA.

SWP-H1295

A family feud...
A dangerous deception...
A secret love...

DESTINY

by Sara Wood

An exciting new trilogy from a
well-loved author...featuring romance,
revenge and secrets from the past.

Join Tanya, Mariann and Suzanne—three very special
women—as they search for their destiny. But their
journeys to love have very different results, as each
encounters the irresistible man of her dreams....

Coming next month:

Book 1—*Tangled Destinies*
Harlequin Presents #1790

Tanya had always idolized Istvan...well, he *was* her brother,
wasn't he? But at a family wedding, Tanya discovered a
dangerous secret...Istvan wasn't related to her at all!

Harlequin Presents: you'll want to know what happens next!

Available in January wherever Harlequin books are sold.

BRIDE'S BAY RESORT

UNLOCK THE DOOR TO GREAT ROMANCE AT BRIDE'S BAY RESORT

Join Harlequin's new across-the-lines series, set in an exclusive hotel on an island off the coast of South Carolina.

Seven of your favorite authors will bring you exciting stories about fascinating heroes and heroines discovering love at Bride's Bay Resort.

Look for these fabulous stories coming to a store near you beginning in January 1996.

Harlequin American Romance #613 in January
Matchmaking Baby by Cathy Gillen Thacker

Harlequin Presents #1794 in February
Indiscretions by Robyn Donald

Harlequin Intrigue #362 in March
Love and Lies by Dawn Stewardson

Harlequin Romance #3404 in April
Make Believe Engagement by Day Leclaire

Harlequin Temptation #588 in May
Stranger in the Night by Roseanne Williams

Harlequin Superromance #695 in June
Married to a Stranger by Connie Bennett

Harlequin Historicals #324 in July
Dulcie's Gift by Ruth Langan

Visit Bride's Bay Resort each month wherever Harlequin books are sold.

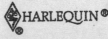

HARLEQUIN ®

BBAYG

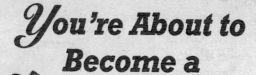

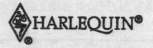